I spent the res... ... ...n doing my dad cho... —laundry, dishes, cleaning, paying bills and yardwork. Even though our friends liked to kid me about how easy I had it, I was pretty good at managing the household. Julianne would even admit it, if she had to. I didn't just lie around the house, eating ice cream and napping. I didn't want Julianne coming home and feeling like she had more to do in the evenings, so I made sure the house was in shape when she got home.

Unless I'd needed a nap.

But as I was working my way through my to-do list, I couldn't get my mind off Moises Huber and the money. He was accused of stealing nearly six hundred thousand dollars. That wasn't twenty bucks out of someone's wallet. That was the kind of money that got you sent to prison. And no matter how sneaky he thought he might've been, there was no way for that amount of money to go missing and people not to take notice. He had to know it wouldn't take long for people to connect him to it, particularly when he had access to it.

It made no sense. If he was dumb, he never would've been in the positions he'd been in to manage the money in the first place. So I didn't buy the idea that he was just stupid. If you were going to blatantly steal money from right under someone's nose, there was usually one big reason.

Desperation.

More Stay at Home Dad Mysteries

by Jeffrey Allen

STAY AT HOME DEAD

POPPED OFF

FATHER KNOWS DEATH
(coming soon)

Published by Kensington Publishing Corp.

Popped
Off

Jeffrey Allen

KENSINGTON PUBLISHING CORP.
http://www.kensingtonbooks.com

KENSINGTON BOOKS are published by

Kensington Publishing Corp.
119 West 40th Street
New York, NY 10018

Copyright © 2012 by Jeff Shelby

All Kensington Titles, Imprints, and Distributed Lines are
available at special quantity discounts for bulk purchases
for sales promotions, premiums, fund-raising, and educa-
tional or institutional use.

Special book excerpts or customized printings can also
be created to fit specific needs. For details, write or
phone the office of the Kensington special sales manager:
Kensington Publishing Corp., 119 West 40th Street,
New York, NY 10018, attn: Special Sales Department,
Phone: 1-800-221-2647.

Kensington and the K logo Reg. U.S. Pat & TM Off.

ISBN-13: 978-0-7582-6690-3
ISBN-10: 0-7582-6690-1

First Mass Market Printing: September 2012

10 9 8 7 6 5 4 3 2 1

Printed in the United States of America

Popped Off

1

"The King of Soccer is missing," Julianne said into my ear.

I was standing on the sideline, sweating, concentrating on the swarm of tiny girls chasing after a soccer ball. As the head coach of my daughter's soccer team, the Mighty, Fightin', Tiny Mermaids, it was my sworn duty to scream myself silly on Saturday afternoons, hoping they might play a little soccer rather than chase butterflies and roll around in the grass. As usual, I was failing.

I gave my wife a quick glance. "What?"

"The King of Soccer is missing," she repeated.

Before I could respond, my five-year-old daughter, Carly, sprinted toward me from the center of the field, ponytail and tiny cleats flying all around her.

"Daddy," she said, huffing and puffing. "How am I doing?"

I held my hand out for a high five. "Awesome, dude."

She nodded as if she already knew. "Good. Hey, are we almost done?"

"About ten more minutes."

She thought about that for a moment, shrugged, and said, "Oh. Okay." Then she turned and sprinted back to the mass of girls surrounding the ball.

Except for the ones holding hands and skipping around the mass of girls surrounding the ball.

I took a deep breath, swallowed the urge to yell something soccer-ish, and turned back to Julianne. "What?"

She was attempting to smother a smile and failing. "Sorry. Didn't mean to interrupt the strategy session, Coach."

"Whatever."

She put her hand on my arm. "I was trying to warn you. Moises Huber is missing."

Moises Huber, aka the King of Soccer, was the president of the Rose Petal Youth Soccer Association. He oversaw approximately two hundred teams across all age groups, close to two thousand kids, five hundred volunteers, and about a billion obnoxious parents.

He was also a bit of a jerk.

"Missing?"

"Hasn't been seen in three days, and Belinda wants to talk to you about it."

I shifted my attention back to the game. Carly broke free from the pack with the ball and loped toward the open goal. My heart jumped, and I moved down the sideline with her. "Go! Keep going!"

Several of the girls trailed behind her, laughing and giggling, not terribly concerned that they were about to be scored upon.

Carly approached the goal, settled the ball in

front of herself, shuffled her feet, and took a mighty swing at the ball.

It glanced off the side of her foot and rolled wide of the goal and over the touchline.

My heart sank, and the gaggle of parents behind me in the bleachers groaned.

Carly turned in my direction, grinned, and gave me a thumbs-up. I smiled back at her through the pain and returned the thumbs-up.

She sprinted back toward her teammates.

Maybe we needed to practice a little more.

I walked back up the sideline to Julianne. "Why does she want to talk to me about it?"

"I think it has to do with you being a superb private eye and all," Julianne said.

"I'm not a private eye."

"Those fancy cards you and Victor hand out beg to differ, Coach."

After successfully proving my innocence in the murder of an old high school rival, I'd reluctantly joined forces with Victor Anthony Doolittle in his investigation business. On a very, very, very limited basis. We were still trying to figure out if we could coexist, and the jury was still deliberating.

I frowned. "What does *missing* mean? Like he's not here today?"

Julianne shrugged. "Dunno. But you can ask her yourself." She tilted her chin in the direction of the sideline. "She's coming your way, Coach." She kissed me on the cheek. "And don't forget. We have a date tonight."

"A date?" I asked.

"Well, a date sounds classier than using you for

sex," she said, slipping her sunglasses over her eyes.
"But call it what you like. Coach." She gave a small
wave and walked away.

I started to say something about being objectified—
and how I was in favor of it—but Belinda Stansfield's
gargantuan body ate up the space Julianne had just
vacated.

"Deuce," Belinda said in between huffs and puffs.
"Need your help."

Her crimson cheeks were drenched in sweat, and
her gray T-shirt was ringed with perspiration. Actually, it appeared as if all 350 pounds of Belinda were
ringed in perspiration.

She ran a meaty hand over her wet forehead and
smoothed her coarse brown hair away from her face.
She took another huff—or maybe it was a puff—and
set her hands on her expansive hips.

"Middle of a game here, Belinda," I said, moving
my gaze back to the field, which I found far more
pleasant. "Can't it wait?"

"No can do, Deuce," she said. "This is serious
business."

Carly tackled one of the opposing girls, literally
threw her arms around her and took her to the
grass. They dissolved into a pile of laughter as the
ball squirted by them.

"Um, so is this, Belinda."

"Oh, please, honey," she said, shading her eyes
from the sun. "These little girls care more about
what's in the cooler after the game than the score.
And these parents don't know a goal from a goose.
You are a babysitter with a whistle. Get over yourself."

Couldn't have put it better myself.

"What's up?" I asked.

"Moe's done and gone and disappeared."

"Like, from the fields?"

"Like, from Rose Petal."

Tara Little started crying and ran past me to her parents. We were now down a Fightin' Mermaid.

"Since when?"

"Today's Saturday," she said, swiping again at the sweat covering her face. "Last anyone saw him was Wednesday."

"Maybe he went on vacation," I said.

"Nope."

"Maybe he's taking a long nap."

"Deuce. I am not kidding."

The pimple-faced referee blew his whistle, and the girls ran faster than they'd run the entire game. They sprinted past me to the bleachers, where a cooler full of drinks and something made entirely of sugar awaited them. Serious soccer players, these little girls.

I took a deep breath, tired from yelling and baking in the sun, and adjusted the visor on my head. "Okay. So he's missing."

She nodded, oceans of sweat cascading down her chubby face. "And there's something else you should know."

I watched the girls, red-faced and exhausted, sitting next to each other on the metal bleachers, sucking down juice boxes, munching on cookies, and swinging their legs back and forth.

There were worse ways to spend a Saturday.

"What's that?" I asked.

"Seventy-three thousand bucks," Belinda said.

"What? What are you talking about?"

She shifted her enormous body from one tree stump of a leg to the other.

"Moe's missing," Belinda said. "And he took seventy-three thousand dollars with him."

2

"All the summer and fall registration fees," Belinda said. "Gone."

The girls were now chasing one another, the parents were chatting, and Belinda and I were sitting on the bottom of the bleachers.

"How is that possible?" I asked. "He just walked away with that much in cash?"

"The bank accounts are empty," she said. "They were full on Tuesday. Before he disappeared."

"Could be a coincidence."

"And I could be a ballerina," she said, raising an eyebrow. "It ain't a coincidence, Deuce."

No, it probably wasn't a coincidence. She was right about that.

"Don't you guys have some sort of control in place for that kind of thing?" I asked. "I mean, with the accounts. Multiple signatures or something like that?"

She shook her head. "Nope. Last year, when Moe was reelected, he demanded full oversight. The board didn't like it, but he said he'd walk without it. So they gave it to him."

"Why did he want it?"

"No clue."

I spied Carly attaching herself to Julianne's leg. She was crying. Carly, not Julianne. Crying had become common after soccer games, the result of too much sugar and some physical exertion. It was less about being upset with something and more about it just being time to get home.

"I want to hire you, Deuce," she said. "We want to hire you. The board. To find him and the money. You and that little dwarf, or whatever he is."

A smile formed on my lips. I wished Victor was there to hear her description of him.

"I'll need to talk to Victor," I told her. "The little dwarf. To make sure he's okay with it."

"You two got so much work you're turning away business?"

As a matter of fact, we did. Or rather, Victor did. Since our initial escapade, people had been seeking us out left and right. My agreement with Victor allowed me the flexibility to work only when I wanted to. Fortunately, he'd been more than capable of handling most of the work and I'd been left alone to play Mr. Mom to Carly.

"No," I said, attempting to be diplomatic. "But we don't take anything on unless both of us agree."

She thought about that for a moment, then nodded.

Then her stomach growled.

"There's one more thing," she said.

"What's that?"

"We can't pay you."

I pinched the bridge of my nose. "That's gonna

be a problem, Belinda. The little dwarf likes money. He tends not to work without it."

"I mean, we can't pay you up front," she clarified. "Everything we got, Moe took. You find him and the money, we'll pay you whatever we owe you."

I knew Victor was going to have a coronary over that.

"I'll talk to Victor and see what I can do," I said, standing.

She pushed her girth up off the bleachers, wobbled for a minute, then steadied herself. She wiped a massive hand across her wet brow.

"Well, I hope you can do something, Deuce," she said, a sour expression settling on her face. "Because that money? That's all we got. It doesn't come back, soccer don't come back."

"Really?"

"We are totally fee driven. Nothing in reserve. So unless you wanna foot the bill for uniforms and trophies and field space and insurance and who the heck knows what else, we need that money."

I glanced over at the remaining girls. Carly had detached herself from Julianne and was now playing some bastardized version of tag. Her team wasn't very good at soccer, but that didn't stop me from espousing the virtues of team sports at a young age. They weren't winning games, but I believed they were getting something out of playing.

"Why would he take the money, Belinda?" I asked.

"I got no idea," she said, shaking her head. "I really don't, Deuce. But we gotta have the money back. Now him?" She waved a hand in the air. "I couldn't care less whether that weasel comes back."

"Weasel?"

Her eyes narrowed. "You don't know him all that well, do you?"

I shrugged. I knew him from around town and from soccer meetings. A little pompous, but other than that, I didn't think much at all about him.

"No," I admitted. "I guess not."

"Weasel," she said. "Pure weasel."

"Why's that?"

"Because that's the way the good Lord made him," she said, frowning. "Or Satan. Whichever."

"So you aren't surprised he took the money, then?" I asked.

"I'm a little surprised," she said. "Because I didn't think even he'd pull something like this. But you know what's more surprising?"

I looked past her. Julianne now had Carly in her arms and was waving at me. I was ready to go home and be objectified.

"Uh, no. What's more surprising?"

She hiked up her ill-fitting shorts and looked me dead in the eye.

"That no one's killed that weasel yet."

3

"You're kidding, right?" I asked as I loaded the soccer gear into the back of the minivan. Julianne and Carly were already settled in their seats. "Why would anyone want to kill Huber?"

"I'm just sayin'," Belinda said in between huffs and puffs, "he's not the most liked fella around Rose Petal."

"A lotta people aren't the most liked, Belinda. That doesn't mean they have a hit out on them."

She shaded her eyes from the sun, a drop of sweat hanging from the tip of her nose. "Lotsa reasons. A biggie?" She leaned closer to me, and I tried not to shrink away. "He cheats at poker."

"What?"

"Poker. He cheats."

I closed the back of the minivan. "What are you talking about?"

"Don't you play in one of them games? Where all you daddies get together and pretend to be manly and play poker?"

I did, in fact. Last Friday of every month. A tight

group of friends, we rotated homes and played until the wee hours of the morning, drinking beer, making fun of one another, and taking each other's money. It was less about the poker and more about the need to do some serious male bonding. Kind of like the kids and their soccer, but with more cursing and beer.

"Well, he used to play in a regular game," Belinda said, "but they found out he was cheating. Kicked his butt out."

"If it was anything like my game, you're expected to cheat."

She shook her head. "No. This was different. They played for stakes bigger than your daughter's lunch money." She nodded, as if confirming to herself what she was saying was true. "Ask around. You'll find out."

I knew that was true. Rose Petal wasn't big, and nearly everyone knew something about someone else's business. It was a fishbowl of sorts. And I had to admit as she was telling me this, I was surprised that I hadn't heard some version of Huber's cheating already.

"I'll get back to you, Belinda," I said, pulling the keys out of my pocket. "No promises, though. I have to talk to Victor first."

"I'll sit on him," she said.

"Huh?"

"I'll sit on that little man if that's what it takes to get him to agree," she said.

"I'll pass that along."

Belinda waddled away across the now empty parking lot, as everyone else had packed up and gone

home. I slid into the driver's seat, shoved the key
into the ignition, and fired up the air-conditioning.

"She is a large woman," Julianne said.

"And then some."

"She wants you to look for the King?"

"Yes."

"And you said?"

"That I had to talk with Victor first."

I backed out of the stall and headed out of the lot.
I glanced in the rearview mirror. Carly was red-faced,
and her eyes were glazed over. She was exhausted.
Which meant a nap was on the horizon. Which
meant . . .

"We may get some alone time," Julianne whispered.

"Was just thinking the same thing."

"You sure you aren't too tired, Coach?" She
moved her hand and rested it on my thigh.

I smiled. "I'm so irresistible, aren't I?"

She lifted her hand. "I just need you to make the
next baby. You're a conduit."

I glanced at her, and she wore the smirk she
always wore that put me in my place.

We were ready for another child. We'd relished
the first five years alone with Carly, and we'd done
that on purpose. She was our first, and we wanted
to dote on her, give her as much attention as possible. And we wanted to be rested before the second
one came along. Not that Carly was a tough kid—she
wasn't—but any child will wear you out as he or she
goes from infancy to toddlerhood to kindergarten.

People looked at us a little strangely. In Rose Petal
you were expected to follow one kid with another,
and then maybe another, so that your house was

filled with small people all under the age of five. But Julianne and I had stood our ground against the peer pressure and had stuck to our plan.

However, it was time to enact phase two of our plan. Which, you know, I was kinda looking forward to. I wasn't going to mind if it took a while. Practice makes perfect.

I pointed the minivan in the direction of our home and tried to obey the speed limit. This was a hard thing to do, particularly when I saw Carly nod off in her car seat.

"She's out," I whispered.

"I know," Julianne whispered back. Her smirk morphed into a smile, and my foot slammed harder on the accelerator.

I slowed down enough so as not to cause the van to go airborne as we pulled into the driveway, and eased it into the garage. I kept the engine running until the garage door was down behind us, then shut off the ignition. Carly wasn't exactly a light sleeper, but she didn't need a lot of encouragement to wake up, either.

"I'll run her upstairs," I said.

"I'll be in the living room."

"The living room?"

The smile grew devilish. "We can be a little . . . noisier in the living room."

Oh, my. "I'll meet you there."

I managed to open the van doors, remove Carly from her seat, and get her into my arms without her stirring. I gave Julianne a thumbs-up, turned, and walked as quickly as I could into the house, up the stairs, and into her room. I laid her down on her bed and she squirmed a little, settling onto the blankets, but kept her eyes shut, smacking her lips.

I paused and smiled. It would be nice to have another of those. I liked being a dad. Even better, I loved being a dad who got to stay home with Carly, far more than I ever anticipated I would. Everyone had warned me that adding a second child to the mix might change my mind, but I was willing to take that chance.

If only because phase two sounded like so much fun.

I bounded down the stairs, careful to keep my footsteps light. I kicked off my sneakers, tossed my socks on top, and found Julianne stretched out on the sofa.

In black lingerie.

"Whoa," I said.

The devilish smile returned. "Such a way with words."

"Whoa," I said again.

"Good thing I don't need to be wooed."

"I could try and woo you."

"Come closer and whisper your woos in my ear."

I leaned down and stretched out my body on top of hers, every synapse in me firing like pistons in a race car. I felt sorry for those men who got bored with their wives. Julianne was more attractive now than the day I met her, and every time she smiled at me, butterflies still took off in my stomach.

She wrapped her arms around my neck and kissed me, setting off fireworks inside my head. Our bodies meshed together, and I realized there was no possible way phase two could ever be overrated.

"Don't you two have a bedroom?" a voice said from the entryway.

Julianne's body stiffened beneath me, and the fireworks in my head disappeared, replaced by a gathering fury that could be brought on by just one person.

"Don't stop on my account," the voice said. "I'll wait till you're done."

"What is he doing in here?" Julianne whispered, shrinking beneath me.

"I have no idea," I said, resting my forehead against hers. "Do we have to stop?"

"Deuce!" Julianne said in my ear. "Do something!"

I sighed and swiveled my head in the direction of the other, unwelcome voice.

Victor Anthony Doolittle waved his tiny fingers at me.

Friggin' midget.

4

I shooed Victor outside so Julianne could get out from beneath me and scamper upstairs to get dressed. I took a couple of deep breaths, clenched and unclenched my fists, and walked out to the front porch.

Victor was sitting on the bench swing, legs a foot off the ground, sipping a Dr Pepper.

"Really," he said, grinning, "you didn't have to stop on my account."

"What the hell are you doing walking into my house uninvited?"

He shrugged. "I knocked. You didn't answer. I walked around back. Back door was open. I was thirsty." He shrugged his shoulders again. "I was gonna walk back out, but then I saw you and the luscious missus about to get down and dirty, and . . . I musta forgot to walk out." He smiled and bounced his eyebrows.

"Do not walk into my home uninvited again. Ever," I said, leaning against the wooden railing that encircled the porch. "Got it?"

He rolled his eyes. "Settle down, Kareem. No way I was gonna stand there and watch you get naked."

"Ever."

His eyes widened, like he couldn't figure out why I was so angry. "Fine. But you should lock your doors, pal."

My fists tightened into balls, something that happened quite frequently when I was around Victor Anthony Doolittle. Every time I saw him, I contemplated ending our little partnership.

Pun intended.

I took a deep breath. "Why are you here?"

"I need a reason?"

"Absolutely. And most of the time, that isn't enough."

"You're starting to hurt my feelings."

"Like you have feelings."

He held the soda can to his lips. "Good point." He tilted his head back, emptied the can, and ripped off a huge belch, crumpling the can in his fat little hand. "I got a call."

"A call?"

"Some woman about some soccer guy? Said she spoke to you?"

I should've known Belinda wouldn't wait. "Belinda."

"That's it, Kareem. Yeah, Belinda. What's the deal?"

I explained what Belinda told me about Huber.

Victor took that in and made a noncommittal face. "Doesn't sound that complicated. Doubt he'd be hard to find."

"Probably not," I agreed.

"Any reason we shouldn't do it?"

"The fact that working with you makes me wanna vomit?"

"Again. The feelings."

"You said you don't have any."

"Oh. Right. So maybe just stop being a jerk, then."

"Where do you get jeans that small? The Children's Place?"

His face flushed and I smiled. He could pretend all he wanted, but cracks about his size always produced a rise. Which almost made it worth him showing up.

"Ha-ha, Kareem," he said, struggling down from the swing and setting his feet on the porch. He was barely bigger than Carly, even with the fedora on his bald head. "Okay. You wanna tell her we'll take it, or you want me to call her?"

"You sure you wanna do it?"

"Sure. Seems like a piece of cake."

"You tell her what our rate is?" I asked.

"Of course."

"And she said?"

"No problem."

I laughed. "She doesn't have any money, Victor."

"Excuse me?"

"Huber took all the money. Literally all of it. She wants to pay us when we find him. *If* we find him. And the money."

"Well, forget that," he said, waving a dismissive hand in the air, his facial features scrunching up with irritation. "That ain't gonna fly."

"Oh, it's gonna fly, Victor," Julianne said, stepping through the screen door and out onto the porch, a T-shirt and shorts now hiding the lingerie. "It's gonna fly."

Victor quickly removed his hat and cupped it to his stomach. "Well, hello, Julianne."

He'd had a crush on her since the moment he'd laid eyes on her, and while it annoyed the crap out of me, I'd been willing to leverage that on several occasions, as had Julianne. He was hard to ruffle, but he came undone anytime she was around.

"Hello, Victor," she said, folding her arms across her chest. "It'll fly. You're taking the case."

"Ma'am?"

"I'm not your mama, so don't 'ma'am' me," she said, wrinkling her nose. "You and Deuce are going to help Belinda."

"We are?" Victor said.

"We are?" I repeated.

She glanced at me, a warning to keep my mouth shut, then moved her gaze back to Victor. "Yes. You are."

"But if she can't pay, then . . ."

"Carly plays in that soccer league, and while I think it just might be the dumbest thing on this planet to chase around a ball, kicking it into some oversize net, she loves it," Julianne explained. "I mean, she lives for it. And if Mr. Huber took all that money and doesn't come back, she isn't going to get to play. And that will make me very unhappy. Do you understand, Victor?"

His cheeks flushed. "Well, yes, ma'am, but—"

"Seriously, honey, if you call me ma'am again, I will break one of your itty-bitty fingers," she said, smiling much the way I imagined pit vipers might smile if they could smile.

His cheeks went from pink to red. "Okay . . . Julianne. But if she can't pay—"

"Victor, honestly," she said, cutting him off again. "You just saw me almost naked. Isn't that payment enough?"

I brought a hand to my mouth to hide a smile.

"And I'm sure you can understand how upset I am that not only were you in my house without permission, but you also interrupted my afternoon with my husband," she continued. "You got to see me in my underwear, but I didn't really get what I wanted."

"Yeah, that's—" I started.

"Shut it, Deuce," she said, without looking at me. "So don't you see, Victor? You owe me."

"I do?" he asked.

"Oh, most definitely. So as payment, I would like for you and Deuce to help Belinda." The pit viper smiled again. "Because otherwise, I will be very, very angry with you. And I don't think you want that."

Victor's mouth tightened into a knotted swirl, and he stared down at the hat in his hands. He shifted his feet against the porch. Finally, he set the hat back on his head.

"Okay," he said. "We'll do it."

Julianne clapped her hands together. "Excellent! I knew you'd see it my way."

Victor nodded, then shook his head like he wasn't sure what had just happened.

I knew the feeling.

"I'll call you," he said, stepping past me and heading down the steps to the sidewalk.

"Oh, and, Victor?" Julianne called, stepping over to the railing.

He stopped and turned around. "Yeah?"

"If you tell anyone that you saw me in my undies, I will stick my fingers so far into your eyes, you'll never see anything ever again." A wide smile settled onto her face. "Okay, sweetie?"

He pursed his lips and nodded his head before getting into his car and driving off.

5

Before we could even attempt to reestablish the mood, Carly stumbled down the stairs.

"I'm hungry," she said, rubbing her eyes.

Julianne swept her up, kissed her cheek, and carried her into the kitchen.

It would've been incredibly sweet if I wasn't so incredibly worked up.

Phase two was put on hold for the rest of the day.

I spent the rest of the afternoon mowing the lawn, washing the cars, and cleaning out the garage in an attempt to burn off my phase two energy. Carly came out and helped me weed along the fence in the backyard, ripping up handfuls of stems, leaving the roots firmly in place.

We finished and, hot and flushed, changed into our swimsuits and walked down to the community pool with Julianne. I commandeered two chaise lounge chairs beneath the awning, while Carly scrambled into the shallow end, already spotting friends to play with.

"Brainstorm with me," I said to Julianne.

She shifted in her chair. "I'm sunning myself."

"Multitask."

"That's what I do during the week."

"Jules. Please."

She sighed. "Fine. How can I be of service?"

"Why does Moe Huber walk off with that money?"

"He wanted to buy a lot of doughnuts?"

"Very funny."

"I don't know him, Deuce," Julianne said. "I have no idea."

I watched Carly cannonball into the water and doggy paddle back to the wall. "Debt. Maybe he owes someone money."

"See? You don't need me."

"Jules."

She sighed and propped herself up on her elbows, keeping an eye on Carly in the water. "All right, all right. Yes, debt would make sense. Probably the first reason anyone steals money. Unless you're Robin Hood."

A beach ball bounced across the surface of the water.

"So maybe he's Robin Hood," I said. "Stealing to help someone."

Julianne wrinkled her nose beneath her oversize sunglasses. "Nah. You don't steal that much if you're giving it to someone else. I like debt better."

"So how does one accrue the kind of debt that would cause one to clean out the coffers of a youth soccer association?"

She swung her legs over the side of the chair and sat up. "A long-building debt? Like it started small and grew. Like you weren't prepared for the hole you dug yourself?"

I thought about what Belinda had told me about poker games.

"Gambling?"

"Sure," she agreed.

I glanced at the water. Carly was splashing water over the side of the pool. "Some sort of get-rich-quick scheme?"

"Okay."

"Drug problem?"

"Maybe."

"What do you think?"

"Isn't this what you're supposed to do as a P.I.?" she asked, an eyebrow arching above the glasses. "Are you putting me on retainer?"

"Jules, I'm being serious."

She held up a hand. "Okay, fine. You can't take a joke this afternoon. I can see where missing out on sex with me might do that to you."

A smile found its way onto my lips.

Carly materialized at our chairs, hugging another little wet girl.

"Audrey's here!" she squealed.

I smiled. "Yes, she is. Hi, Audrey."

"Hi!"

They were preschool pals. They could've been twins and had a penchant for hugging one another as tightly as they could.

"Can Carly come to my camp?" Audrey asked.

"Please!" Carly said.

"What camp?" Julianne asked.

"At my church. VBS!"

"Please!" Carly said again.

Julianne glanced at me. "It's okay with me."

"We'll see," I said.

Carly frowned. "When will we see?"

"We'll see," I repeated.

"When?"

"Carly."

"Please, Daddy."

The word *Daddy* had a profound effect on me. In that it usually caused me to acquiesce.

"Okay," I said, shaking my head. "We'll figure it out."

They started jumping up and down and headed back to the water.

"You are such a pushover," Julianne said, smiling.

"Here's where I'm stuck," I said, watching Carly grab onto the metal railing that descended into the water, then spin herself upside down on it like a monkey. "Belinda said Huber insisted on full financial oversight, giving him the power to do whatever he wanted without having to involve anyone else."

"Right. Unbelievably stupid and irresponsible on the association's part."

"Yeah. But that was almost a year ago when he was reelected."

Julianne eyed the pool and rested her chin in her hand. "So it was something he was planning."

"Or there was something he was already into and he was worried that it was going to get out of hand."

"You really don't need me for this," she said, smiling.

"You make me feel smart."

"I seek to serve."

"So then where does he go with the money?"

She thought for a minute. "To whomever he owes it to. Or to hide. Or to Jamaica."

"Maybe I'll need to go to Jamaica to look for him."

"Or maybe just send Victor."

"Not sure he's capable of handling that trip alone."

"Not sure you'd have a wife to come back to if you went to Jamaica without her." She stood. "I'm hot. I'm getting in the water."

"That much cash is a lot to travel with."

"Probably didn't fit in his wallet, no."

"That's what I'm saying," I said. "Physically, that is a lot to carry."

Julianne leaned down and set her hands on my shoulders. "You don't need me. Hash it out with Victor. He's unbelievably annoying, but he's actually good at this. Don't forget that."

I nodded. He really was. For all the hair he made me want to pull out, Victor really was good at investigating. I'd never say it out loud, but he was better than I was.

Julianne leaned down and kissed me. "And don't forget to help me make a baby tonight, after Carly goes to sleep. Get all your hashing out done before you get naked."

She sauntered off to join our daughter in the pool.

6

We returned home to find my parents sitting on the front porch, huddled together, staring intently at a laptop.

My father looked up as we approached. "Oh, thank God you're finally home."

My mother's face took on a grave expression. "We need your help, Deuce."

I glanced at Julianne, who stared worriedly at them.

"What's the matter?" I asked. "What is it?"

My father threw up his hands, then shoved the laptop over to my mother. "This stupid Facebook! It makes no sense!"

I exhaled, relieved that no one was dying.

We ushered them into the house, and while Julianne and Carly went to the kitchen, I settled onto the sofa with my parents.

It was great living so close to them in Rose Petal. Most of the time. They were terrific grandparents and never failed to help out at a moment's notice. They lived to spend time with Carly and were dropping not-so-subtle hints about child number two. We were happy to help them out, as well, when they needed it. Watching their house when they went on vacation. Helping my dad with projects. Normal, everyday things that we most certainly took for granted.

But technology . . . well, technology, I was afraid might be the end of all of us.

It had started with cell phones. They were vehemently opposed to them. We finally convinced them that if they were going to watch Carly for us, they needed to have a cell phone. So we got them one. Just one. Which they didn't share, because my dad refused to learn how to use it.

And they were resistant to computers. They didn't see the need for e-mail and the Internet. At least until Carly came home and said she wanted to send them an e-mail. They went shopping for a laptop the next day.

So now they had caved under the peer pressure that can only be created by fellow grandparents looking to brag about their grandchildren. Which meant they were attempting to integrate themselves into Facebook.

It wasn't going well.

"Okay," I said, kicking off my sandals and settling into the sofa. "What's the problem?"

My father made a face. "Facebook is the problem."

My mother frowned at him, then looked at me. "Well, I have a few questions."

"Okay."

"This news feed thing," she said, much in the same way someone might say "snake" or "feces." "It's trying to tell me what to do."

"No, it's not, Mom."

Frustration screwed up her face. "Well, not tell me what to do, but it wants me to comment on the things my friends have put on here."

"Right."

She looked at me nervously. "What happens if I don't?"

"Don't comment?"

"I don't want everyone in the world reading what she has to say," my father piped in. "No reason for that!"

"Well, if you don't comment, they will take away your Facebook account and they might come take your computer."

My mother sat up straighter.

"Like hell they will," my father said, raising an eyebrow. "Any of them Facebook fellas show up at my door and try to take away my computer . . ."

"Dad, I'm kidding," I said before he laid out his entire plan to defend his home from the evil Facebook fellas.

My mother stared at me disapprovingly. "Deuce."

"If you don't want to comment, Mom, then don't."

"I don't have to?"

"No."

"But the box is there, telling me to comment."

"You don't have to."

She exchanged a look with my father, skeptical and nervous.

Social media was not created to cause this kind of anxiety.

"Well, how do we block everyone from seeing what she wrote?" my father asked.

"You can't. If you post a comment on someone's wall, all their friends can see it."

"We don't know all their friends."

"So?"

"So they don't need to be reading what your mother is writing."

"What exactly is she going to say, Dad?"

"Her comments!"

I took a deep breath and tried to remember how foreign this was for them.

"Let's say your friend posts a picture of a new grandbaby," I said.

"Lorraine," my father said with a sneer. "That woman thinks all her grandkids are like gold bars. She'd absolutely post a picture. Even if the kid looks like a possum."

My mother nodded in agreement.

"And let's say that, for once, you decided to be polite," I continued. "And you decided to say something like 'He's so cute' or 'She's adorable.'"

"Fat chance unless you like possums."

"Right. But we're pretending that you are normal and civil and don't tell people their grandchildren look like rodents."

My father rolled his eyes. "Fine."

"So if you said something like that, why would you care if anyone else read that?" I asked.

They again exchanged anxious looks, before my mother said, "Well, I don't know."

"It's like being at a cocktail party," I explained, trying to find a comparison that would resonate. "You're just having polite conversation. So as long as you are polite, it doesn't matter who reads what you write. You aren't giving out your bank account information or Social Security numbers."

"But what if someone does ask for my bank account information or Social Security number?" Mom asked.

"Say no."

She stared at me, completely puzzled.

"Mom, you don't have to do anything you don't want to," I said. "If you just want to view other peoples' pictures or what they have to say, that's fine. You don't have to do anything. I promise."

"I wanna block people," my dad said. "I got a list."

"They've probably already blocked you, Dad."

"They better not have!"

7

My parents stayed awhile longer, mercifully occupied by Carly rather than the nuances of social networking. Julianne invited them to stay for dinner, but my mother had left something in the oven before the Facebook emergency led them to our home, so they politely excused themselves.

We ate dinner in quiet, all three of us worn out from the afternoon in the heat and water. I took Carly upstairs for her bath while Julianne cleaned up the kitchen. Carly's eyes closed as soon as her damp hair hit the pillow. I planted a kiss on her forehead and clicked off the light.

I dialed Victor as I collapsed onto my own bed.

"Doolittle. Go."

"You are ridiculous."

Victor was not amused. "What do you want?"

"I have a question for you."

"Go."

"Do you just lay your phone on the floor? Because if you tried to put it up on a counter or table, I don't see how you'd get it back."

The click was loud in my ear, but worth it.

I dialed again.

"Look, Winters, if you're just calling to make short jokes, you can shove them up your—"

"Easy. I'm just messing with you. I actually have a real question."

"Make it fast, moron."

"I don't know Huber at all. Where do we start?"

I could almost feel him smile through the phone. "Oh. So you need my help now?"

My joke seemed less funny now. "I suppose."

"You suppose. I wanna hear you say it."

"It."

"Try again, funnyman."

I clutched the phone in my hand and silently cursed my big mouth. "I need your help."

"Why?"

I swallowed hard. "Because I don't know where to start on a guy I know nothing about."

His chuckle resonated through the phone. "I just recorded that."

"Whatever."

"That'll come in handy someday."

"You gonna answer my question or not?"

He cleared his throat. "You start digging."

"Digging?"

"Yeah. We gotta get a picture of him before he disappeared. Doing that will help us know where to look."

"What if it doesn't?"

"It will."

"But what if it doesn't?"

"It will."

I rolled my eyes at his confidence. I didn't think it

was that easy. And God help me if he ended up being right.

"Okay," I said. "So where do we start digging?"

"Friends. Family. Coworkers. We'll get his phone records. E-mails. It ain't that hard. Even for a bozo like you."

He made it sound easy, but I wasn't so sure.

"So here's your first assignment," Victor said. "Start poking around all those soccer people. Find out who saw him last. Who talked to him last. Whose Facebook wall he posted on last. All that crap. You do that and I'll give you a gold star."

"Do you pay full price at the movies?" I asked. "Or do you get the kid discount? And do you use those plastic booster seats so you can see over normal-sized people?"

The click seemed even louder this time, and that pleased me.

I lay on the bed for a few minutes, enjoying my juvenile humor, then pulled out my laptop from the bottom of my nightstand. I lifted open the top and found my way to Facebook.

I was indifferent toward Facebook, and most of the time I felt like the only one. All my friends were on it constantly, and Julianne rarely went more than, oh, six minutes without checking it on her phone. I found some things funny and enjoyed seeing the pictures that other people posted, but I didn't feel the need to share every moment of my life with my so-called friends.

But I wondered if Moises Huber did.

I logged into my dusty account and typed his name into the search bar.

The third profile that popped up was for a Moises Huber in Rose Petal.

Investigating was apparently easy.

I clicked on his profile, and the entire thing opened. Nothing tucked behind any sort of privacy setting. Julianne, ever the lawyer, was always yelling at me about my privacy settings, but given that I didn't post anything of significance, I couldn't have cared less who was looking at my pages. It seemed far too complicated to figure out how to throw up walls.

Although I assumed my father would have it figured out soon.

The profile picture was of a soccer ball. It listed his birthday as August 3 and his relationship status as single. He had 247 friends. I recognized a few of them. He liked to play one of the Mafia games that made no sense to me but that I was always being invited to play.

I clicked on his wall, and his activity seemed sporadic. He'd post a couple of times in a day and then disappear for a week. He seemed to be a casual user, much in the same way that I would log on if I was on the computer, but made no concerted effort to do so otherwise.

I looked at the last post.

It was from four days ago, which would've been a day before anyone last saw him.

See you tonight! someone named J. MacDonald had posted. **We'll have a blast!**

J. MacDonald's profile pic was of a bald eagle, which I was sure had some significance to J. Mac-Donald, but none to me. I scrolled down the page to see if MacDonald was a regular poster on the wall, but I didn't see anything else.

I clicked on J. MacDonald's profile, but this person was apparently very familiar with Facebook's privacy settings. I got a message stating that J. MacDonald shared information only with friends.

So there.

"Are you asleep?" Julianne called from the hall.

"Nope. On Facebook."

"Oh." She stepped into the doorway. "Maybe I shouldn't interrupt you."

I looked up from the computer.

She was back in the black lingerie. She'd added black, thigh-high boots.

She perched a hand on her bare hip. "I can leave if you'd like. . . ."

"No!" I said, pushing the laptop onto the floor.

I was willing to risk computer damage for phase two.

8

Julianne was out of bed before I was Monday morning, and I woke alone, tangled in the sheets, her black lace bra draped strategically across my forehead.

My wife. Lawyer. Mother. Seductress.

She and Carly were both in the kitchen when I wandered downstairs. Carly smiled at me as she worked on a piece of toast. Julianne stared into her oatmeal, perplexed.

"Daddy's up!" Carly yelled. "Lazy pants!"

"Easy." I ruffled the top of her head. "Your mom kept me up late last night."

I looked for a reaction from Julianne, but she continued eyeing her oatmeal.

"I have swimming today, Daddy."

"I know."

"I'm gonna do a cannonball. Okay?"

"Absolutely," I said, sliding into the chair between them. I nudged Julianne. "Good morning."

She set her spoon down next to her bowl and folded her arms across her chest. "I'm not pregnant."

"How do you know?"

"Because I know."

I lowered my voice. "We just had sex last night. How can you possibly know?"

She looked at me, annoyed. "A woman knows these things."

I knew better than to argue. "All right."

"Why is it taking so long?"

"I kinda like that it's taking a while."

Her lips puckered. "Didn't take this long before."

I could see her thoughts developing, and it sent chills up my spine. She was about to embrace her own special tunnel vision with regard to getting pregnant. I tried to stave it off.

"We haven't been trying that long, Jules," I said. "Really."

"I think we need to get serious about this."

I swallowed. "Get serious?"

She leveled her eyes with mine. "Yes."

Julianne was a lot of things, and nearly all of them were fantastic. Better than I deserved. But she was also a perfectionist, and she didn't tolerate failure. Ever. I beat her at Scrabble one time. She wouldn't play with me again for a month. Then she suggested we play.

She won by 271 points. Because she'd spent the month reading the Scrabble dictionary.

She didn't lose and she didn't fail.

"What's pregnant, Daddy?" Carly asked, stacking her bread crusts on her plate.

"It's when you have a baby," I said.

"Mommy's gonna have a baby?" she said, grinning. "Yay!"

Julianne stood, took her bowl to the sink, then turned back to face me. Her expression was a mixture of resolve and grim determination, similar to what I imagined the leader of SEAL Team Six's looked like right before they stormed bin Laden's hideout. "Yeah. Mommy's gonna have a baby."

It was time to get serious.

9

Carly cannonballed straight into the pool for her swimming lessons, soaking the instructor and her classmates and earning a stern talking-to from the now doused instructor. She snuck a look back at me through the window to the waiting room where I sat to see if she was in trouble.

I winked and gave her a quick thumbs-up.

I had forty-five minutes to kill while she learned the finer points of swimming like a human rather than a puppy dog. As usual, I was the only male in the room, the rest of the waiting parents being moms who were either just coming from or on their way to spinning class or a tennis match or whatever else the moms of Rose Petal did during the day. I was an anomaly in Rose Petal—a father who stayed at home—and was regularly viewed with a raised eyebrow whenever I ventured somewhere new during a time of the day when most other dads were at a desk.

But I'd been a regular at the swim school now for a while, and the staff and the parents were used to seeing me sit and watch and make polite chitchat. So they left me alone and didn't feel the need to call the police and alert them that a pedophile might be on the loose.

I was scrolling through e-mails on my phone when the door to the waiting room opened. Victor Anthony Doolittle strode through it, acting like he owned the place. He eyed several of the women, then settled on me and found his way over.

"You take your kid to an indoor pool? In Texas?" he asked.

"Yes. Because one hundred and twelve degrees is not a comfortable temperature to learn in."

"Sissy."

"What are you doing here?" I asked.

"Looking for you," he said, dragging a chair up next to mine and climbing up into it.

"I hope the front desk didn't think you were late for class."

"You're so funny, I forgot to laugh."

"No one says that anymore."

"I just did, ya moron."

I shook my head. "What do you want? And how did you know I was here?"

He made a face as if I'd peed on his shoes. "Please. I know your schedule better than you do. I can find you anytime I need to."

"Lucky me."

"I know your wife's, too," he said, raising an eyebrow and grinning.

I reached over and tilted the chair back, threatening to let it go to the floor. He fell back in the seat and braced himself with his hands. "What the—"

"Do not talk about Julianne," I said. "You know the rules. You ogle my wife, I will hang you from a nail somewhere."

"All right, all right," he said, still bracing himself. "Set the chair back down, and calm down."

I set it down.

He ran his tiny hands over his shirt and rolled his eyes at me. "Can't take a joke at all anymore."

"Why are you here?"

"Got a little bit on your missing soccer coach."

"He's not a coach. He's the president"

"Whatever. Soccer is for Euro pansies, anyway."

I sighed and watched Carly dive into the pool. Her arms chopped through the water like windmills, and she was first to the opposite side.

"So this Huber," Victor said. "I got into his e-mail."

"Already?"

He waved a hand. "Getting into someone's e-mail is child's play."

"No wonder it's so easy for you."

"Har, har. I got into his e-mail. I figured you might wanna take a look."

"You see anything in it?"

"No. Because I didn't look. That's your job."

"Okay."

He produced a stapled packet of papers. "I printed them all out. If there's an address that isn't familiar, shoot it back to me. I'll figure out who it belongs to."

I took the stack of paper and fanned the pages. There looked to be about thirty pages worth of material.

"Your kid can swim," Victor said.

I glanced up. They were now racing the length of the pool, and Carly was ahead by about three body lengths.

"She's pretty good," I admitted.

"Probably your wife's genes."

He was trying to get a rise out of me, and I wasn't going to give him the pleasure. "Probably."

He waited for me to say something else, but I stayed quiet. He fidgeted in his seat for a moment, looking uncomfortable and irritable. Though you could argue that was how he always looked.

"She a good sleeper?" he asked. "Your daughter?"

"Yeah, pretty good."

"What about when she was a baby?"

"Oh, hell no. She was awful."

"What did you do?"

I started to respond, then caught myself. "Are you asking for my help?"

He scowled but kept his mouth shut.

"Baby not sleeping, Victor?"

He put his head in his hands. "I swear to God, if he doesn't sleep tonight, I'm taking him back to the hospital and getting a kitten or something. Kid hasn't slept in a week. And neither have we!"

Victor and his wife had a three-month-old, Victor Junior. He hadn't said much about the baby since he was born, and I hadn't pried. It wasn't like we hung out together and babysat each other's kids, so I didn't know much about Junior.

"Say it," I said.

"Say what?"

"Say you need my help," I said, smiling.

His cheeks flushed as he remembered our conversation from two nights ago He mumbled something under his breath, then coughed. "Fine. I need your help."

I let his words settle between us for a moment, relishing the feeling of a petty and juvenile victory. Still, it felt good.

"Do you swaddle him?" I asked.

"What him?"

"Swaddle. Wrap him up in a blanket."

"No. She's afraid it'll freak him out or something."

"Do it. Wrap him up. Tight."

He stared at me for a minute, attempting to decipher whether or not I was being honest with him.

"I'm not kidding, Victor," I assured him. "And I may like to give you a hard time, but I wouldn't tell you to do anything that would harm your son."

His expression softened, and I could make out faint dark circles beneath his eyes. The badges of honor for new parents.

"Lay him on the blanket," I explained. "Get his arms flat to his sides, and pull the blanket over him. Tuck the blanket around him, like a burrito. And you can't do it too tight."

"What if he can't breathe?"

"Promise you, he'll be able to breathe."

He pursed his lips. "I don't think it'll work."

"I'll bet you a case of beer it does."

He hopped out of the chair. "Deal. I like Shiner."

"And I'll take Stella," I said. "Bottles, not cans." I grinned. "It'll work."

He lifted his chin in my direction. "The e-mails. Check the e-mails."

"Why?"

"You may find some things."

"I thought you said you didn't look at them."

He headed for the door. "I say a lot of things, Stilts."

10

Before I could skim the e-mails, Carly bounced out of the pool area, needing a towel and dry clothes. I supplied both, and we were out the door in less than ten minutes, as I didn't feel the need to stand there and brush out her hair and make her pageant ready, like the other parents did with their children.

"Daddy, we're going to camp now, right?" Carly asked, chomping on a bagful of Cheez-Its I'd brought along for quick nourishment.

"Yep."

"At that church, right?"

"Yep. At that church."

"That church" was one of the mega-sized churches that seemed to pop up daily in the Dallas suburbs. I was pretty sure the only thing people in Texas liked more than barbecue was going to church. Julianne and I were indifferent to them—except when they created traffic and we were trying to go out to breakfast on a Sunday morning—but Carly hadn't stopped talking about going to that church since Audrey invited her to attend vacation Bible school.

Vacation Bible schools were a tradition in the South, and they were less about the Bible than they were about being summer camps. Swimming, games, sports, and crafts, all sprinkled with a generous dusting of Jesus. And they were usually dirt cheap. So as long as Carly wasn't being brainwashed by some sort of religious cult, I didn't mind her spending a few hours at a VBS.

I pulled the minivan into the massive parking lot of New Spirit Fellowship Church. When I say massive, I mean the size of about three football fields. The church itself was more of a campus, with numerous buildings, fountains, athletic fields, and the massive main church, all metal and glass with high-angled rooflines. It was an impressive structure, and I was pretty sure that, like Cowboys Stadium, it was large enough for God to spot from Heaven.

We walked into the mammoth vestibule. A long table was set up, with a bevy of smiling faces behind it, beckoning us in. We stepped up to a lady wearing a giant smile and a pink baseball cap with a bejeweled cross on it.

"Well, good morning!" she greeted us. "How are we today?"

"We are fine," Carly announced.

Pink Cross Hat directed her energy at Carly. "And are we ready for camp?"

"Yes, we are."

"And are we ready to have a fantastic time?"

Carly turned to me. "Daddy, why does she keep saying 'we'? I don't even know her."

I wanted to tell her because people thought using

the first person was a cute way to build camaraderie, but that it just made people sound silly. I refrained.

"Probably because she's part of the camp," I told her. I looked at the woman. "Last name is Winters."

Her smile did not fade at Carly's interrupting her cavalcade of we's, and she pressed on. "Well, of course you are." She scanned the list and her finger stopped. "There we are. Miss Carly Winters."

Carly beamed.

"And is Audrey Risberg here yet?" I asked. "They're buddies, and Audrey invited her to come this week."

She scanned the list, then shook her head. "No, it doesn't appear as if she's here yet. But I'm sure the Lord will have her here any moment!"

I pictured the Lord pulling up in a minivan. I wondered if the Son of God would prefer a foreign or domestic model.

The woman handed Carly a name tag and a bright red T-shirt that exclaimed SUPER SUMMER FUN TIME! The letter *T* was in the shape of a cross. I felt my skepticism rising at being surrounded by all this religion but managed to keep my mouth closed.

She pointed in the direction of Carly's group leader, and we weaved our way through the crowd of parents and children. The leader's name was Elizabeth, and she was an older teenager sporting the same T-shirt Carly had just been handed. She welcomed Carly like she'd known her forever. She shook my hand, told me where the pickup location was, and returned her attention to the kids clamoring around her. Carly gave me a quick kiss good-bye and began chattering with the other kids.

I worked my way back through the crowd, toward

the table and Pink Cross Hat. She was making nota-
tions on the list.

"Excuse me," I said. "I'm sorry to bother you
again."

She lit up with a megawatt smile. "It's never a
bother when you're serving the Lord. And that's
exactly what I'm doing with all these wonderful little
people!"

"Right, absolutely," I said, biting my tongue and
swallowing the thirty-seven sarcastic answers that
formed in my narrow-minded brain. "Was wondering if you might be able to help me find someone
who works here at the church."

The smile grew impossibly larger. "Sir, I know
everyone that works here. Would you like to speak
to someone in ministry? There is always someone
here to speak with regarding ministry or finding
the Lord."

"No, no," I said, holding her off before she had
me baptized. "Someone specific."

"Who?"

"Moises Huber."

Her smile flickered. If I hadn't been looking for
it, I might have missed it. But the name surprised
her, and the reaction wasn't a positive one.

She shuffled the papers on the table and stood.
"Let me see what I can do. I'll be right back. Mr. Winters, correct?"

I nodded.

She whispered something to one of the women at
the table next to hers, and the woman nodded and
slid over to take over Pink Cross Hat's chair and
check-in duties. She smiled at me but said nothing.

I stepped to the side and watched families roll in

and out for a few minutes. If the day camp was any indicator, the church's membership was thriving. At a time when many religious communities were struggling to survive, this one seemed to be doing just fine. People knew one another, hugged, shook hands, seemed happy to see one another. If they were all showing up on weekends and dropping money in the baskets, New Spirit was more than flush.

Pink Cross Hat returned, the bright smile back on her face. The momentary tick that I'd seen before she left was nowhere to be found.

"Mr. Winters," she said, clapping her hands together. "You are in for such a special treat."

For a moment, I thought I'd hit the jackpot. "Mr. Huber is here?"

"Better!" she said.

"Better?"

"If you'll follow me, please."

"Where are we going?"

She smiled and clapped her hands again. "You'll see."

11

Along our walk out of the church to one of the smaller outer buildings, I learned Pink Cross Hat's name was Marie and she'd been a member of New Spirit since it formed. And it had saved her life.

"Your life?" I asked as we walked.

She nodded enthusiastically. "Yes, sir. I was wandering down the wrong path, and New Spirit swooped in and pointed me down the right one."

"Ah." What else was there to say to that?

"Where do you attend?"

And there it was. In Texas it was as commonplace a question as "Where do you work?" or "Where were you born?" or "How'd you meet your spouse?" "Where do you attend?" Meaning, what church?

"Uh, we don't."

She stopped dead in her tracks. "Excuse me?"

"We don't attend anywhere," I said. "We sleep in on Sunday mornings."

"We have Saturday evening services," she said, completely missing my weak attempt at humor.

"Sure," I said. "It's just not our thing."

She kept her eyes on me, studying me like she'd just found a rare insect in her shoe. "So you don't attend . . . anywhere?"

"Nope."

She blinked several times, trying to process my answer. "Well, that's . . . interesting."

We crossed a massive courtyard, at the center of which stood a fountain, and she punched a code on a panel next to a door to gain entrance to a smaller, more generic-looking building. We went up a short switchback stairway, and she pointed to a massive set of double oak doors.

"Charles would be happy to talk to you," she said, smiling.

"Charles?"

She nodded, then realized I didn't know who she was referring to. She shook her head, a mixture of amusement and disgust on her face. "Our pastor. Charles Haygood."

"Oh. All right."

She was still shaking her head as she disappeared down the stairs.

I knocked on one of the doors, and a voice beckoned me in.

The doors opened to an expansive corner office. There was a small living room set up to my right, with leather sofas and a glass-top coffee table. To the left were four square-back easy chairs arranged around a woven rug. In the center of the room, backed by floor-to-ceiling windows, was a massive desk.

Charles Haygood stood behind the desk. Thick dark hair was swept back above a smooth tan forehead. Bright blue eyes and a blinding smile welcomed me into the room.

"Mr. Winters," he said, hands on his hips. "Nice to see you. Welcome."

He was handsome, but I couldn't help but think he looked like a figure from a wax museum. He was fit, well dressed, and a little stiff.

He came around the desk, and we shook hands. He gestured to the four chairs, and we each took one, sitting across from one another.

"Your daughter is here for camp, I understand," he said, settling back and folding his hands in his lap.

"Yeah. First time."

"She'll have a great time."

"I'm sure."

"Have you been to New Spirit before?"

"I have not."

His smile widened. "The Lord brings us people every day."

"My Honda brought me here."

He laughed, a little too enthusiastically. "Of course. Forgive me. But it would be a pleasure if we could persuade you to attend one of our services. I think you might enjoy it."

"I appreciate the invitation."

He rubbed his chin, nodding, momentarily placated. "So . . . you asked about Moises?"

"Yes."

He stared at me, committing to nothing.

My natural inclination was to continue babbling, but one of the things Victor was adamant about was that you learned more when you shut your mouth and stayed patient. Neither was my strong suit, but I'd seen that philosophy in action and it worked. I couldn't argue.

So I waited.

Haygood crossed his legs and readjusted his hands. "Technically, he is still employed here."

"Technically?"

He uncrossed his legs and shifted his weight in the chair, like he couldn't get comfortable. "We haven't seen him in several days."

"Why's that?"

He tented his fingers in front of his chest. "Why are you asking, Mr. Winters?"

"I've been hired to find him, ask him a few questions."

"You're an investigator?" he asked, raising an eyebrow. "I thought you were a football coach or something."

"I'm both," I answered.

He thought about that, then nodded. "I see."

I thought it was interesting that he knew I coached football. I begrudgingly admitted that many folks still knew me from my high school playing days, but I didn't think he was around back then. I let it go for the moment.

"So you haven't seen him in several days?" I asked.

"Correct."

"How many is several?"

He raised his eyes to the ceiling for a moment, then brought them back to me. "Six, I believe. Six."

"He hasn't called in sick?"

"No."

"No call at all?"

"None."

He was playing cat and mouse with me, but I wasn't sure why.

"Can I ask what position he holds here?" I asked.

The lines around Haygood's eyes tightened. "He worked in accounting."

"Doing?"

He cleared his throat. "As our controller."

Another connection to money. Maybe Victor was right. This didn't seem so hard.

"May I ask why you are looking for him?" Haygood questioned, rubbing his chin.

"Because he's missing."

He cracked an insincere smile. "Yes. Of course. Any other reason?"

"I can't really say. It's a private issue."

He stared me down for a long minute, his eyes locked onto mine, maybe waiting to see if I'd break.

I didn't.

He finally nodded. "Understood."

"Has he ever taken off before?"

He shook his head, smiling. "No. He was a very good employee, actually. Started as a part-time worker, worked his way up."

"I assume you've attempted to reach him."

Yes. I went to his home myself to see if I could . . . locate him."

I found it a little strange that Haygood had gone looking for him, but I didn't think it was totally out of the ordinary. If the church was a tight-knit community, I could see them taking care of their own. Worrying about their members.

"I've been there several times, in fact," Haygood said. "To his home."

"Several times?"

"Yes."

"You must be worried."

The corners of his mouth twitched. "Yes. I am."

"About Huber? About what might've happened to him?"

He took a deep breath and blinked several times, then set his hands on his knees. "I'm more worried about the half a million dollars he stole from me."

the corners of his mouth twitched. "Yes, I say.
"About Hébert." About what might've happened
to him.

He took a deep breath and blinked several times,
then set his hands on his knees. "I'm sure worried
about that, a million dollars bleeding from me.

12

"Technically, it's not my money," Charles Haygood explained. "It belongs to the church. But I'm responsible for it."

He'd gotten up and poured himself a glass of ice water from a pitcher on a shelf across the room. He came back and sat down without offering me any.

"We called him the first day when he didn't show up," he explained, holding the glass between both of his hands. "No answer. Not a huge concern. Maybe he's really sick, unable to get to the phone."

I nodded.

"But then he never called back," he said, raising an eyebrow. "That seemed . . . odd. Especially from him. Like I said, never a red flag before."

He sipped from the glass, then went back to squeezing it. "So we called again. No answer or response. So we sent someone over to his home. No answer there either." His lips tightened. "Then we realized the money was gone."

"How?"

"End-of-the-day accounting," he said, shrugging.

"We have a routine process. Checks and balances. Nothing special, but routine things that we do to keep our books in order. Much of our money comes from cash donations at our services, so we are careful and detailed."

I figured there was probably a great deal of cash coming in based upon the campus of New Spirit and the size of Haygood's office.

"At the same time we were calling the authorities to do a welfare check on his home, I was informed that the money was no longer in the account," he explained. His fingers were white, wrapped tightly around the glass. "We did our due diligence and realized that it had been withdrawn the previous evening."

"He had the ability to clear that much on his own?" I asked.

"No. I believe he forged the second signature." His entire face tightened. "Mine."

"Wow."

He nodded grimly. "Yes. This is the kind of thing that brings churches down, Mr. Winters. Destroys them. I am concerned for the members of this community."

Not to mention, you know, himself.

"Did you know him well?" I asked.

"Well enough. We didn't socialize, but he was a regular here at New Spirit. Showed up at our services and our events. As the controller, he and I worked closely together on financial matters. It's my church. I'm responsible for it in all ways. So I can be a bit . . . detail oriented." He flashed a thin smile. "Probably micromanaging most of the time."

I appreciated that he could admit his flaws. He

wasn't coming across as arrogant or entitled. He seemed genuinely concerned for the well-being of the entire church, as well as himself. Despite my skepticism, I liked him.

"So my guess is that perhaps you are looking for him for similar reasons," Haygood said.

"Perhaps."

He nodded, believing he was correct. Maybe knowing. I wasn't exactly known for my poker face.

"Have you reported the theft to the police?" I asked.

He hesitated, then shook his head. "No."

"Why not?"

"I can't afford the attention," he said, shifting uncomfortably in the chair. "If anything about this gets out, the church and the community will suffer."

"I understand that. But that's a lot of money."

He stared at me for a moment. "Yes. It is. So we are working on it . . . independently."

"Independently?"

"Much like whoever your client is, I suppose. We are attempting to locate him without involving the authorities yet."

"We?"

Haygood stood. "Mr. Winters, I'm sorry I couldn't be of more help."

I stood as well. He wasn't going to answer my questions, and he was done with me. He hadn't gotten anything from me, and he was frustrated.

Maybe I didn't like him, after all.

We walked toward the door.

"I do hope that if you locate him, you'll let me know," he said.

"I'll do what I can," I answered because I wasn't going to promise him anything.

Haygood nodded and we shook hands.

"The Lord works in mysterious ways," he said. "I'm sure He will help us locate Mr. Huber." His eyes narrowed. "And will administer to him him any punishment he deserves."

13

I made my way out of Haygood's office and the outer building and headed back toward the church, seeking both a bit of air-conditioning and a few minutes to process my conversation.

I didn't think Haygood knew where Huber was, but I definitely got the impression that he knew more than he was letting on. And the way he'd talked about looking for Huber creeped me out. I wasn't sure if he had some sort of Jesus posse out there looking for him, but I felt certain that he had something cooking. And Huber would be the main course if they found him.

The cool air-conditioning cascaded down on me as I reentered the church. The check-in tables had been pushed aside, and the masses of children were gone, herded off to classrooms and play areas. It looked like a church vestibule again—quiet and orderly.

The walls were lined with glass-framed photos, and I walked closer to them, partly out of curiosity and partly because I wasn't quite ready to venture back out into the heat. The photos were of church-sponsored events—picnics, baptisms, fund-raisers, holiday services.

The next-to-last photo caught my attention, because Moises Huber was in the middle of it.

"Can I help you, sir?" a voice asked from behind me.

I turned around. An older woman with gray hair and a pleasant smile stood there with her hands behind her back.

"Oh, I just dropped off my daughter at the VBS," I said.

"Excellent," she said. "She'll be well taken care of."

"I'm sure." I gestured to the photos. "These pictures are terrific."

She stepped closer and adjusted the glasses on her face. "Oh, yes. We usually have a photographer at every New Spirit event. We like to document the memories."

I pointed at the photo of Huber. "This looks great. What was it?"

She leaned closer. "Oh, that's our annual Casino Night." She grinned at me. "Of course, it's all with play money, and the donations collected are spread throughout the families in need here at New Spirit."

"Wow, that's great," I said. "This guy in the picture, he looks like he's having a good time."

"Ah, yes," she said, nodding. "Mr. Huber. He's been here awhile."

"Has he?"

"Well, I think so. I'm just a volunteer. But I see him quite often."

"That right?"

She nodded, certain. "Oh, yes. As a matter of fact, if I'm not mistaken, he was in charge."

"In charge?"

"Yes, sir. Of Casino Night. He's organized it the last few years."

I glanced at the photo. He had his arms around two people, a man and a woman, big fuzzy dice in one hand and a red plastic cup in the other. A crooked smile slithered across his face, his dark hair slightly askew.

"He's the reason Casino Night is such a success," she said.

"Really? How's that?"

"Why, he organized all the games."

"The games?"

"The casino games," she said. "Blackjack, poker, some other card games I'm afraid I don't know much about."

That was interesting. "Really? He's the guy?"

"Oh my, yes. They had a hard time making any money at Casino Night. It's somewhat expensive to stage, and no one here had the know-how to put it all together. So it was actually costing us money to put it on."

"What kind of know-how?" I asked, looking at the photo.

"Someone who understood casino games," she answered. "And Mr. Huber is apparently an expert."

14

I spent the rest of the morning and the afternoon doing my dad chores—laundry, dishes, cleaning, paying bills, and yard work. Even though our friends liked to kid me about how easy I had it, I was pretty good at managing the household. Julianne would even admit it, if she had to. I didn't just lie around the house, eating ice cream and napping. I didn't want Julianne coming home and feeling like she had more to do in the evenings, so I made sure the house was in shape when she got home.

Unless I'd needed a nap.

But as I was working my way through my to-do list, I couldn't get my mind off Moises Huber and the money. He was accused of stealing nearly six hundred thousand dollars. That wasn't twenty bucks out of someone's wallet. That was the kind of money that got you sent to prison. And no matter how sneaky he thought he might've been, there was no way for that amount of money to go missing and people not to take notice. He had to know it wouldn't take long for people to connect him to it, particularly when he had access to it.

It made no sense. If he was dumb, he never would've been in the positions he'd been in to manage the money in the first place. So I didn't buy the idea that he was just stupid. If you were going to blatantly steal money from right under someone's nose, there was usually one big reason.

Desperation.

After I put the final load of laundry away, I still had a little time before I needed to pick up Carly at camp. I sat down at the kitchen table with a Diet Pepsi and the e-mail printouts Victor gave me.

There were about thirty pages in the stack, with multiple e-mails on each page. I put the total number of e-mails to read at somewhere near a hundred. Most were innocuous and didn't tell me much. Confirmations of soccer games, church events, receipts for bill payments. Nothing that raised a red flag. And that really wasn't surprising. I figured he didn't use his personal e-mail address for work-related business, especially since it pertained to finances.

I was about ready to throw them in the trash when something on the next-to-last page caught my attention.

The e-mail was from an Elliott Huber.

Hey, cuz! the e-mail read. Looking forward to seeing you this week. I signed you up for the weekend tourney. I covered your buy-in with my employee discount. Hope you're ready!

The e-mail address was eHuber@comriventertain.
com.

I grabbed my laptop and used Google to search
the domain name in the e-mail address. It came back
as Comanche River Entertainment. There was a link
to the main Web site. I knew the name but clicked
on the link, anyway.

The Comanche River Resort and Casino was one
of a group of casinos near the northern Texas–
southern Oklahoma border. Massive billboards
advertising it dotted the Dallas landscape, offering
gambling and entertainment only ninety minutes
away. Comanche River was one of the biggest. It
boasted a massive casino and a hotel, along with a
theater that regularly hosted top-name country
music acts. They billed themselves as a resort. I'd
been there once, having made a Saturday night trip
up with my poker buddies. It was truly a mammoth
place.

I perused the Web site for a few minutes, seeing if
the name Elliott Huber popped up anywhere. I
didn't have any luck. All I could find were generic
contact addresses.

But I did have another idea.

The Web site worked hard to bring visitors to
the casino and the hotel. It advertised specials
everywhere. I punched in Friday night, and it came
back with a great bargain rate for a night at the
hotel.

I hesitated for a moment. Julianne didn't like
it when I mixed business with pleasure, but I was
thinking that a night away might be conducive to

Operation Baby Making. A little dinner, a little gambling, and a lot of time in the hotel room.

And if I managed to run into any member of the Huber family, well, that would just be a bonus.

I patted myself on the back as I made the reservation.

15

I picked up Carly from camp, and we returned home. She wasn't singing a Jesus song or trying to convert me, so the day was a success as far as I was concerned. She scampered up to her room, babbling something about playing with her dolls. I was pretty good at playing, but I still hadn't figured out the elaborate world she had created with her plethora of dolls.

When I was halfway through tenderizing chicken breasts for the grill, Julianne hustled into the kitchen, hugging two large pieces of white poster board.

She tossed her purse and briefcase on the table but held on to the poster board. "Okay. We're ready."

"Okay. Good. Ready for what?"

"Phase two."

"I thought we were already on to phase two. Speaking of which, I—"

"Oh. Fine," she said. "Phase three. Where's Carly?"

"Upstairs."

"Excellent." She laid the poster board across the kitchen table. "Here."

Both posters were covered with printouts. Dates, percentages, initials, multiple colors.

"What's all this?"

"Phase three."

I looked at her blankly.

She let out an exasperated breath. "Okay. These charts are going to help us get pregnant."

I set down the wooden mallet I was pounding the chicken with. "Charts? What? Do we lie on those things or something?"

"I've calendared the next sixty days," she said, ignoring me and pointing to the dates. "You'll see the next two months are accounted for."

"Because we didn't have a regular calendar?"

"Now, the days in black, we can ignore those. We won't be having sex on those days."

There were an awful lot of black dates. "Excuse me?"

She looked at me. "I won't be ovulating. There's no point."

"No point?"

"You know what I mean." She turned back to the charts. "Now, stay with me. The red days are iffy. We can have sex on some of those days, even though the likelihood of conception is low."

I scanned the posters. "What does green mean?"

"Green means sex," she said. "Those are my optimal days for conception. You can look forward to multiple encounters on those days."

Multiple encounters sounded good. I made a mental note to list green as my new favorite color.

"What do the initials stand for?" I asked. "BBT? CM?"

"Things I need to start charting. Basal body temperature. Cervical mucus."

"Cervical what?" Those were two words I never thought I'd hear spoken in the same sentence. I didn't think mucus even existed in any lower body cavity.

She dismissed me. "It's irrelevant. At least for you."

I scanned the calendars again. "A couple of these green days are during the workweek. . . ."

"I'm a partner. I can be flexible with my hours."

"Or we can do it in your office," I said, winking.

"Yes, absolutely," she said, nodding. "I had Marsha calendar these days on my schedule. We'll work out the locations this weekend."

Marsha was her newest assistant. I wondered what that conversation had sounded like.

"You'll notice the numbers written in the corner of each day," Julianne continued. "Those are the percentages."

"Percentages?"

"Percentages that I might conceive," she said. "Obviously, they are highest on the green days."

"Obviously."

"You see the pink and blue dots?"

Each green day had either a blue or pink dot strategically positioned in the middle of the box. "Yes."

"They indicate the baby's gender."

"What?"

"Some days are better for conceiving boys and vice versa."

"Are we aiming for one or the other?"

She shook her head. "Not really. But it's good to know."

"Can I ask you something?"

"Yes." She continued to study the charts.

"Did you get any work done today?"

"You don't think this was work?" she asked, raising an eyebrow.

"I didn't say that."

"Yes, you just did."

"I meant . . . legal work. As in related to your job."

She dismissed that with a wave of her hand. "Please. I excel at multitasking. This took only a few hours."

"Okay. What if I want to have sex on a black day?" I asked.

"Negative," she said, shaking her head. "There's no point, and we don't want your sperm count dropping."

"No. That would be terrible." I paused. "But there are so many . . ."

She must have noticed the expression on my face. "Don't worry. With all of this planning, I'm confident we'll be pregnant in a month. Maybe two. Then we can have sex whenever you want."

I wasn't convinced.

"I know all of this may seem a bit . . . premeditated."

"A bit?"

"But I plan to excite you with new lingerie and other pleasant surprises." She tapped the poster board. "You won't be bored."

I was beginning to think I'd need a lot of new surprises to counterbalance the black days that loomed large on the calendar.

"Oh! I almost forgot." She shook her head. "No masturbation."

"Jules?"

"We want your sperm count as high as possible at all times."

"Jules?"

"Just for a couple of months, Deuce."

"Jules!"

Her head snapped up in my direction. "What?"

I started to say something sarcastic, something about charts and graphs and premeditation.

But I held my tongue.

She'd gone through a lot of trouble to put this together. No matter how insane I thought it was, this was Julianne. This was her way. This was her telling me how much she wanted a baby.

I walked over and put my arms around her and kissed her cheek. "Okay."

"Okay?"

"Okay," I said. "Whatever you say. Tell me what to do and I'll do it."

"I know."

I laughed and kissed her again. "I know you know. I'm just telling you. And I don't need lingerie or anything else to get excited. You excite me."

"So you don't want lingerie?"

"I didn't say that."

"I didn't think so."

I kissed her again, this time on the lips. I wasn't lying. I didn't need anything to excite me. Julianne still lit my flame, more so now than the day I met her. She was all I needed.

She pulled back and poked me in the chest with her index finger. "I'm serious."

"I know you are. I will abide by the calendar. I won't try to seduce you on black days."

She snuggled into me for a minute. "Not what I meant, but that's good to know."

"Oh. What did you mean?"

"No masturbation."

16

That evening was a black evening, so after dinner we spent the rest of the night playing board games with Carly before turning in. I refrained from making any jokes because I feared she might take a green day away from me.

When we crawled into bed, I told her about going to Comanche River.

"And don't worry," I said. "I already consulted the chart. It's a green night."

She smiled. "That sounds . . . nice. Your parents will watch Carly?"

"Of course."

She pressed into me, her legs entwined with mine. "Then I look forward to a green night with you away from home."

We switched off the lights, and I fought off the guilt about having another motive in going. I rationalized it by telling myself that I probably wouldn't find anything while we were there, that it really would be just about me and her.

I tossed and turned, trying to convince myself.

Julianne was out the door the next morning, just as I was stumbling down to the kitchen. I sat at the table, waiting for the coffeepot to refill—Julianne always emptied an entire one before leaving for the office—and for my eyes to unglue. The laptop was still on the table from the night before, and I pulled up my e-mail.

The usual junk mail was in the folder, but there was also an e-mail from Belinda.

Something else is missing. Can you give me a call when you get this?

She'd sent the e-mail just after midnight.

I wondered what she could've discovered in the middle of the night that necessitated the e-mail.

Carly rushed downstairs hugging about sixteen dolls and stuffed animals, complaining that she was already hungry. I set her up at the table with toast and a glass of milk, then grabbed my cell and dialed Belinda's number.

"You got the e-mail?" she answered.

"Good morning, Belinda."

"Oh, right. Good morning. You got the e-mail?"

"Yep."

"When can you meet me?"

"Uh, I dunno. Meet you where?"

"You know the field house out at Lake Park?"

"The stone building in the middle of the complex?"

"That's the one."

I checked the clock. "An hour or so?"

"Okay. I'll meet you there."

"Wait. Can't you just tell me?"

The line buzzed. "I think you just need to see it. I'll meet you there in an hour." She hung up.

I set the phone down and sighed. I hadn't planned on a trip to the soccer fields. I was hoping for a nice leisurely morning at the pool, with a little grocery shopping mixed in.

But, hey, plans change.

It beat going into an office or not getting to spend the day with my daughter. I needed to keep the complaining to myself.

Carly finished her breakfast and put on a tank top and shorts while I finished my coffee and tossed on a pair of shorts and a T-shirt. I ran a brush through my hair and met Carly back in the kitchen.

"We're going to the soccer field, okay?" I told her.

"Do we have a game today?"

"No."

"Practice?"

"Nope. I need to go see Miss Belinda about something. It won't take long, and then we can come back and swim. It's going to be hot."

She rolled her eyes. "It's always hot, Daddy."

"I know. You wanna take anything with us?"

She dashed up the stairs. She was at the stage where she always had to take a backpack full of stuff with her wherever she went. Stuffed animals, books, crayons, it didn't matter. She needed to have a bagful of things before she'd leave the house.

She bounced back into the kitchen, her pink Hello Kitty backpack strapped across her shoulders. "Okay. I'm ready."

"Got everything?"

"Yes. White kitty, a coloring book, and my bottle of water. From last night."

"Perfect."

We climbed into the van and headed across

town. I wasn't used to morning traffic in Rose Petal, because we rarely had to head out into it. But we hit every light as it turned red, and ended up being ten minutes later than I'd planned.

Lake Park was an expansive athletic complex on the east side of town. It housed eight soccer fields, two football fields, and two baseball diamonds. The older kids played their games out there, so we had yet to have to fight the weekend crowds to get in and out of the complex. I wasn't looking forward to those Saturday mornings.

The field house was in the middle of the soccer fields, a medium-sized stone building that housed a snack bar on two sides, some bathrooms on another, and I didn't know what on the other. The referees always hung out there on hot days, so I'd always assumed it housed a locker room or something similar.

Belinda paced back and forth in front of the door on the mystery side like a waddling walrus. She stopped as soon as she saw us.

"Sorry," I said. "Traffic was bad."

She nodded. "Always is coming this way."

I put my hands on my hips. "So. Why are we here?"

She pulled open the door behind her and waved us in.

It was a large concrete-floored room, maybe twenty-five feet by twenty-five feet. A long folding table rested against the far wall, a group of folding chairs lined up next to it. The rest of the room was empty, and the air was stagnant and warm.

I spun in a slow circle. "Uh, okay."

"We pay to use this space," Belinda said. "We have

to rent it from the city every season, even though we already pay exorbitant fees to use the fields."

"Daddy, it's hot in here," Carly complained.

"We won't be here long," I told her. I looked at Belinda. "Right?"

"During the season, we keep a bunch of stuff out here," Belinda continued. "Cones, jerseys, extra whistles, coolers. Stuff we might need on Saturdays. The officials will change in here, too."

"Okay."

"Daddy, it's *really* hot in here."

"I know, kiddo. Give me just a minute."

She sighed and plopped down on the concrete.

"But near the end of the season, we start clearing it out," Belinda said. "Cleaning it up."

I sighed, frustrated that we weren't getting to the point. "Okay."

"You have a team mom?" she asked.

"Yeah. Sandy Yook. She's awesome."

"She grab your trophies for you?"

"Yep."

Belinda nodded. "She comes here to get them."

"In here?"

"Yeah. We have them delivered here. It's the largest storage space we have access to."

I wasn't getting it. "Okay. Good to know."

"The trophies were delivered last week," Belinda said.

"To where?"

She laughed. "To here."

"Seriously?"

"Thirteen hundred trophies, Deuce," she said. "A

box for every team, a trophy for every kid in the Rose Petal soccer program."

I knew that. It was recreational soccer. No standings or records. Every kid got to play. And every kid got a trophy.

"You know for sure they were delivered?" I asked.

She nodded. "I met the delivery guy here the Saturday before last. Took him an hour to unload them all. The only empty space in here was where that table was set up." She pointed at the table against the wall. "All thirteen hundred trophies. Boxed up and divided by age group and division."

"What are you telling me, Belinda?" I asked. "That they were stolen?"

She laughed. "Well, yeah. But guess what?"

I sighed again. I was tired of guessing. "I don't want to guess."

"Guess who's the only person with a key to this room?"

I thought for a moment. "Moises Huber?"

She nodded slowly. "That's right."

17

We walked out of the building and back out into the morning sunshine and heat. Carly asked if she could go play in one of the massive soccer goals while we talked, and I told her sure. I watched her sprint across the grass.

"Why the hell would he take the trophies?" I asked.

"I really have no idea, Deuce," Belinda said, leaning against the building. "Not a clue."

"They aren't expensive, are they?"

"As many as we buy, they end up being less than a buck a trophy," she said. "It's a minimal cost."

"So what could he possibly do with them?"

"No clue."

"And how would he get them out of here?"

Belinda shrugged. "Guy that delivered them had a twenty-five-foot U-Haul. Big truck."

I nodded. Someone would have noticed a truck like that pulling into Lake Park. Unless it had been the middle of the night.

"Maybe someone broke in," I said.

She pointed at the door. The lock looked perfect.

"Maybe someone else has a key," I said.

"I had to leave my driver's license at the city rec office just to get the key to come over here and show you," she said. "There is one spare key, and Huber has it."

My head hurt. I couldn't put any of it together. The pieces didn't fit. The gambling and the money did, but a bunch of cheap trophies for kids?

That didn't fit.

"Okay," I said. "Can you get me the delivery guy's info? And the contact info for the trophy company?"

"Sure," she said. "But I'm telling you it's him. Huber took 'em."

"How do you know?"

"I just do, Deuce," she said. "Something wasn't right with him the last few weeks. He was acting goofy and nervous. And I'm telling you, no one else could get in here. Who would want them?"

No one I could think of. Most of the coaches complained about even having to pick them up. We avoided it at all costs, cajoling a parent to do it for us. And they were cheap. They'd break at the drop of a hat. So it wasn't like they'd be worth anything on the black market.

No, I didn't have a clue as to what Moises Huber would want with thirteen hundred cheap soccer trophies.

18

We said good-bye to Belinda, and she promised to e-mail me the trophy info I'd asked her for. I really wasn't sure what good it would do me, because I agreed with Belinda. It might not make much sense that Huber took the trophies, but he was the overwhelming choice to have done so.

Carly and I spent the rest of the day at the pool. She'd been good the previous two days, while I'd been occupied with trying to figure out where Huber was, but she was starting to pull a bit more on me, and that meant she needed my attention. She wasn't a high-maintenance kid, and I had learned over the years that if she was pulling on me, it meant that I'd been ignoring her.

So we did cannonballs and got McDonald's for lunch and built a giant Lego farm and ate ice cream and made grilled cheese sandwiches for dinner. Julianne came home to a messy house but laughed when she saw us both with aprons on, covered in melted cheese.

And that was one more reason I loved Julianne.

She didn't complain when things weren't perfect when she came home. She seemed to sense when we needed a totally disorganized day, and was happy to catch the tail end of it.

It was a good day.

As was the rest of the week. We swam. We went to camp. We goofed off. Summers were when I most appreciated being a dad. Schedules went out the window, and I could just enjoy time with my daughter without anything getting in the way.

I poked around, looking for a bit more on Huber, but didn't come up with anything. The Internet gave me nothing, and I couldn't find any other leads. But I'd learned from Victor to be patient. Sometimes the case had to come to you.

Friday morning I dropped Carly at my parents' house. Julianne and I weren't leaving until that evening, but any chance they had to spend with Carly, they tried to drag out for as long as possible.

Carly sprinted out of the minivan and onto my parents' front porch. My dad was in his swinging chair, and she launched herself onto his lap. He hugged her, whispered something into her ear, causing her eyes to widen.

"You offer her cash if she doesn't tell me about all the stuff you buy her this weekend?" I asked, coming up the stairs.

"None of your beeswax," he said, setting Carly down. "What goes on in my house stays in my house."

"We're on the porch."

"Watch yourself. I can still take you out."

"Right."

Carly slithered by me and disappeared into the house.

"Gonna go spend your wife's money at the casino, huh?" my dad asked, raising an eyebrow.

"Shut up."

"Watch yourself."

I leaned against the weathered railing. "We're just going up for the night."

"So nice of her to carry your big butt around like that."

My father never passed up the opportunity to needle me about staying at home. And I never passed up the opportunity to let it stick me.

"Whatever," I said, lacking a better response. "You know anything about New Spirit?"

"The church?"

"Yeah."

"You looking for Jesus?"

"No."

"Maybe the Lord is calling to you?"

"Dad."

He chuckled. Nothing gave him more pleasure than giving me a hard time.

"I don't know much about it," he said. "Know a few people who attend. They seem to like it just fine. Think your mother got invited once or twice. We declined."

My parents were longtime members of the local Methodist church. Asking them to attend anywhere else was like asking them to move to Kenya. Wasn't gonna happen.

"You ever met the pastor?" I asked.

He thought for a moment. "Haywood, right?"

"Haygood."

"Same difference," he said. "Don't think I've ever said hello to him. Seen him around, of course. Can't say I've ever heard anything bad about the man." He studied me. "Why?"

"Just a thing I'm working on."

"Ah. You playing Inspector Clouseau?"

"Ha."

He chuckled again. Small things like bad jokes made his day.

"Just looking for a guy that works there," I said.

"That the soccer fella?"

"Yeah. How'd you know?"

He shrugged. "Aw, ya know. Word gets around."

I shook my head. He and his buddies were like a group of old women. Nothing went on in Rose Petal without them getting wind of it.

"Heard he took a bundle from Carly's soccer thing."

"Looks like he did, yeah."

"Wouldn't be the worst thing in the world if no one played soccer." He wrinkled his nose. "Stupid game."

I was beginning to think soccer was the most hated sport in America. Or at least in Rose Petal. "Your granddaughter would be devastated."

His mouth twisted. "Well, yeah. There's that. But still. There's no scoring. And their socks are too high."

"Good reasons to abolish a sport, Dad."

He leaned back in his chair. "This Huber fella . . . That's the guy, right?"

I nodded.

"He got kicked out of his regular game."

"Regular game?"

My dad nodded. "Poker. And not some sissy game like you play in, where they play old maid, or whatever the hell it is you clowns play."

"We don't play old maid."

"Slapjack, whatever. It ain't poker."

My father's poker-playing sensibilities were offended because we played a whole variety of games based on poker, but they weren't necessarily traditional forms. We invited him one time, and he was horrified.

"So he got kicked out?" I asked, trying to get him back on track.

"Yep, that's what I heard."

"Who played in the game?"

My dad shrugged. "Not exactly sure. Think your neighbor down the way. Guy with the truck."

"Joel?"

"Yeah, think so, but I can't remember."

"Why'd he get kicked out?"

"They got tired of taking his IOUs."

"Really?"

"Really."

"They were playing for that kinda money?"

"Told ya it wasn't the old lady game you play in."

A couple of crows buzzed the porch.

"Yeah, but they played for that kind of money? That required IOUs?"

"Guess so."

The birds buzzed by again. I knew our game was small. We all tossed twenty bucks in and played on that. No one won a ton, but no one lost a bunch, either. It sounded not only like Huber was playing in a game that had high stakes, but also like he was overmatched in it. And if they'd kicked him out, he still owed them money.

Everything kept coming back to gambling and money.

My dad stood and steadied the swinging chair behind him.

"You probably won't like the casino," he said, heading for the house.

"Why's that?"

"They don't have Go Fish."

He cackled all the way into the house.

19

I went home and spent the rest of the day tying up loose ends around the house. Dishes, laundry, bills, vacuuming. Which meant we could come back from Oklahoma to a clean house and not worry about having to do anything. Those were the little things you learned when you stayed at home, but never appreciated prior to that. And those were the things I tried never to say out loud, for fear of losing my man card.

I sent Victor an e-mail telling him about the missing trophies and about the poker issues. I'd held off on telling him because I wanted to see if I could come up with a link myself. It felt like I was always leaning on him to put things together, and it bugged me. I worked them through my head while getting the house squared away, but nothing clicked. It was frustrating. I felt like I'd learned a bunch of new things about Huber, but was nowhere closer to figuring out exactly what was going on with him. The only thing I felt sure about was that he definitely had some money issues. And it sure looked like he had some sort of gambling problem. I could see how that might lead to him stealing money, but I couldn't for the life of me figure out why he might run off with a bunch of crappy trophies.

Julianne came home early, and I pushed the thoughts of Moises Huber out of my head so we could enjoy the two-hour drive north to the Oklahoma border.

Except the traffic out of Dallas on a Friday afternoon was murder, and we ended up doing about fifteen miles per hour for the first hour.

"Have we ever gone to a casino together?" Julianne pondered from the passenger seat as we inched forward in the stop-and-go traffic.

"I don't think so."

"You've been to Vegas without me."

"Yeah."

"You didn't invite me," she accused.

"I believe you said, 'Vegas is filled with hookers and cigarettes. Why would anyone go there?'"

"Still. I didn't receive an invitation."

"It was for a bachelor party," I reminded her.

She smirked. "I'm not debating the reason for the trip. I'm simply pointing out I wasn't invited."

"Well, I know it's weighed on you forever, so that's why I thought I should make up for it this weekend."

"So Comanche River is just like Caesars Palace?"

"Very similar."

"It will sate my desire to go to Las Vegas?"

"Yes. It's exactly like Las Vegas." I paused. "Only in Oklahoma."

"That doesn't sound . . . right."

I laughed. "My only goal is to make you happy and give you what you think you're missing."

She laughed and squeezed my hand.

We drove in silence for a while, the radio playing quietly. It was one of the things I enjoyed most about my wife. She didn't have to make chatter just to hear herself talk. We could sit there and be content with the quiet.

"What do you want to name the baby?" she asked as the traffic started to open up.

"The baby? You're pregnant now?"

"I'm going to be."

"Of course you are. How about we conceive first, then plan the name?"

"Negative, Ghost Rider," she said. "I'm going to be pregnant very soon, so we should start discussing these things."

"Why? You've stated in the past that you have ninety-five percent of the naming rights, due to your ability to carry the child. That leaves me with only an irrelevant five percent."

"True," she admitted. "But I like to make you feel included."

"Fine. Chuck and Sally."

"You aren't taking this seriously." She squeezed my hand tighter. "I'll cut your irrelevant rights to three percent for that if you're not careful."

"Hurt me."

"Names, please, Mr. Driver."

I glanced out the window as we passed the University of North Texas athletic complex. "If it's a boy, Kellen."

"What is a Kellen?"

"It's a name."

"Name of what?"

"A boy."

"And whom else?"

I rolled my eyes. "Jeez, Jules. I dunno. You asked me for a name. I gave you one."

"You know, it's harder for me to conceive if I'm stressed out."

She was switching tracks faster than a race-car driver.

"Uh. Okay."

"And right now you're not doing much to keep my stress levels down when I'm trying to talk to you about the baby."

"Maybe we should stop for beer."

"Alcohol is actually a conception inhibitor. So no."

"Wait." I glanced in her direction. "You won't be drinking tonight?"

"No."

"What if I wanted to have drunk sex with you?"

She leaned over in the seat and placed her hand on my thigh. "I don't need to be drunk to be fantastic in bed."

I swallowed. "I know."

Her fingers dug into my thigh. "Do you?"

"Yes, ma'am."

"You shouldn't drink, either," she said. "It lowers your sperm count."

"I like it when you talk dirty."

Her hand slid higher on my thigh, and my spine straightened.

"Just wait till we get there," she purred.

20

The Comanche River Resort and Casino looked like a castle. Only bigger. Four huge spires jutted into the sky, each one made up of neon lights that could be seen for miles. There were multiple entrances and a parking lot roughly the size of Delaware. Rows and rows of cars filled acres and acres of asphalt. It was like pulling into Disneyland for adults.

In Oklahoma.

Rather than try to find a parking spot, I headed for the valet line. They whisked our bags out of the car and escorted us into the castle.

The incessant ringing of slot machines assaulted my ears as soon as we stepped inside. My feet sunk into the plush red carpeting as we walked toward the check-in desk. There were people everywhere—in lines, in groups, in pairs. Comanche River didn't seem to have trouble attracting visitors.

The polite clerk behind the check-in desk handed us our room keys and casino cards and pointed us in the direction of the elevator. Our room was on the tenth floor and was less tacky than I expected. The room was expansive, easily accommodating a four-poster king bed, and the furnishings were deep, dark wood. There was a sitting area near the window with a small love seat and a coffee table. The window looked out to the back of the property, a mix of huge oak trees and wild grasses that cascaded down to a small creek.

"This is not what I expected a casino hotel room to look like," Julianne said, looking out the window.

"I know. I'm kind of impressed."

She walked toward me, kissed me on the cheek, and said, "Me, too."

She then went past me, grabbed her bag, threw it on the bed, and immediately began unpacking.

"Only took fourteen seconds," I said, throwing my bag on the bed next to hers.

"Making fun of me increases my stress levels, Deuce," she said as she methodically removed her clothes and inserted them into the hotel dresser. "Not good."

Not once in her life had she ever left clothes in a suitcase or duffel bag. Didn't matter where we were. She didn't even take her shoes off before the bags were unpacked.

She moved over to my bag and unzipped it. "I don't think you want me to blame you for our inability to conceive. No telling what I might make you do."

She had a point.

"Are you going to shower?" I asked.

"Duh."

Julianne Rule #2. Always shower the second you get to a hotel room.

No, I don't know why. I just know that's the rule.

"All right, well, how about I go find us some food and bring it back to the room?" I said. "Unless you'd like me to join you in the shower . . ."

"That would be lovely." She put the last of my clothes into the drawer and threw her arms around my neck. "The food, not the shower. Let's do the joint shower . . . later. And thank you for arranging this."

"You're welcome."

She kissed me. "I hadn't said thank you yet. I'm glad to be here with you."

"Me too."

"And we are so gonna make a baby."

She kissed me, and her lips lingered on mine. I felt the familiar desire bubble up. I was thrilled to be spending a night in a hotel with her, alone, just the two of us.

She patted my chest with her hand. "You have thirty minutes. Go find food, and play one of your little gambling games if you must." A slow smile spread across her face. "I'll be waiting."

I flew out the door.

21

In the half hour we'd been upstairs, the population in the casino seemingly doubled. It was wall-to-wall people.

The casino itself was like the largest convention hall you could imagine. The gaming tables were lined down the middle of the room, surrounded by all shapes and sizes of slot machines advertising different jackpots, bonus games, and trademarked themes. The exterior was ringed with money windows, bars, and restaurants. It was sensory overload at its finest.

I wound my way through the throngs of people and found a pizza place with a short line. I ordered a pizza, a salad, and a couple of iced teas. They told me it would be about thirty minutes, but since we were staying in the hotel, they'd be happy to deliver it to the room. I gave them the room number and headed back out to the casino floor.

In truth, I had no idea what I was doing. I had all sorts of ideas running through my head, but I didn't have a clue as to how to go about investigating any of them. I suddenly felt stupid for having brought Julianne up here under false pretenses. It seemed juvenile and pointless.

Frustrated and chagrined, I decided to find a blackjack table to kill a few minutes before heading back up to the room. I didn't want to take my frustration back with me. I might not have been totally honest about my reasons for wanting to come up here, but I could make sure we still had a good time, and I didn't want to drag anything negative into the baby-making plans.

Negativity was most likely a sperm inhibitor.

A chair opened up at a five-dollar table at the end of a row, and I sat down, buying forty bucks' worth of chips. Four senior citizens occupied the other chairs, a man and three women. They didn't even acknowledge me, enamored with the colorful stacks in front of them.

The dealer nodded at me. Female, younger than me, with a long ponytail, dark skin, and a dimpled chin. Her name tag said JASMINE.

Jasmine dealt cards down the line, and I hit blackjack with a ten of diamonds and the ace of hearts on the draw. The seniors scowled at me as Jasmine doubled my chips on the bet line.

"Beginner's luck," I said, shrugging my shoulders.

The seniors grumbled among one another and replaced their bets.

This time I drew a seven and a six. I asked for another card and received an eight.

"What the hell?" said the woman to my immediate right.

"We been sittin' here for an hour and haven't

seen no cards like that," said the woman down on the end.

"Sorry, ladies," I said, placing another bet. "It won't last long."

But it did. I won eleven consecutive hands. The old ladies couldn't take it any longer and struggled out of their chairs and moved away, mumbling something about fixes and the dealer.

"Didn't mean to run off your business," I said to Jasmine.

She smiled and ran the cards through the shuffler. "That's all right. They're regulars, and they're never happy."

I'd already tripled my money, so I rolled her a ten-dollar chip. "Thanks for the cards so far."

She removed the chip from the table. "Thank you, sir. Continue?"

"Absolutely. Until my luck disappears."

She smiled. "We'll hope it lasts."

No one filled the seats down the line, word apparently getting out that I owned the table.

"So those ladies are regulars?" I asked.

Jasmine dealt me a ten and an eight. "Oh yes. Every weekend. From somewhere in Oklahoma. Tulsa, maybe."

I waved a hand over the cards, declining another. Jasmine drew an eight and an eight and then a six.

Twelve in a row.

I set my winnings on the bet line.

"You work every Friday night?" I asked.

She threw me a nine and a six. "Yes, sir. And Saturday. Busiest nights of the week."

I considered my fifteen for a second, weighing the odds and whether I should take a hit. I decided to motion for another card. She passed me a three, and I stayed. She busted out again.

Thirteen in a row.

I tried not to think about it.

"You worked here awhile?" I asked, repositioning the chips on the bet line.

"Almost two years."

"You like it?"

She smiled. "It's a job. I'm a grad student in Norman. Physics."

"And you're doing this?"

"Pays better than anything else you can find. Trust me."

I nodded.

She dealt me a seven and a four. I signaled for another. She dealt me the ten of spades.

Fourteen wins.

"Though I don't think it pays what you're making tonight," she said, gathering the cards and handing over my winnings.

I rolled another ten bucks back to her.

"Thank you, sir."

"You're welcome."

"Continue?"

"I haven't had this kinda luck since I met my wife. So yes."

She smiled and nodded.

I played for another twenty minutes. I lost one hand. I had started on forty bucks and was now up over five hundred.

A small crowd had gathered behind me, watching the win streak and murmuring. No one sat down, not wanting to change the rhythm or my karma, I guess.

"You know a lot of the other folks that work here?" I asked as she dealt me a four and a nine.

"What do you mean?"

"Your coworkers. Do you get to know them, or do you know the customers better?"

Jasmine drew a nine and an eight for herself. I signaled for a card, and she dealt me a five. I held at eighteen.

"A few," she said. "But I don't stick around. Too busy with school."

She drew a six for herself, and the dealer busted again.

The crowd behind me rippled.

I kept my winnings on the bet line. "You don't by any chance know someone by the last name of Huber, do you?"

Jasmine thought for a moment, then shook her head. "Don't think so. You have a friend that works here?"

"Oh, no," I said. "Just . . . It's a long story."

Two men in suits had materialized to my left and were now watching us intently. Or rather, me.

Jasmine dealt me a five and four. She drew a nine and a ten. I waved for more cards.

Four. That gave me thirteen to her nineteen. I needed another card.

Six. Tied at nineteen. Should I chance it? Why not?

Two. I smiled at the twenty-one.

The crowd rippled again, and the two suits frowned.

Jasmine set my winnings in front of me. I glanced at my watch. The pizza had probably been delivered fifteen minutes ago. I needed to go.

I laid fifty dollars in chips in front of Jasmine and

stood. "Thank you. I'm gonna quit before it all comes back to haunt me."

Her easy smile was gone now, but she forced one onto her face. "Thank you, sir. Enjoy the rest of your visit."

I gathered my chips and headed for a cage.

The two suits split, one staying at the table and one following me. I was almost to the change cage when he tapped me on the shoulder.

"May I have word with you, sir?" he asked.

"Sure," I said, continuing to walk.

"Would you mind coming with me?"

"Uh, actually, yes. I would."

I reached the cage and set my chips on the ledge. "I'd like to cash in, please."

The gray-haired woman behind the counter started to reach for the chips, but the suit put his hand on them. "One moment, Doreen."

Doreen immediately pulled back from the counter.

"Is there a problem?" I asked.

"Would you mind following me, sir?"

"We already covered that. Yes. I would."

The suit had small eyes and a small mouth made smaller by his large triangular nose. The mouth twisted.

"And you should probably take your hands off my chips," I said. "Because they're mine."

The suit lifted his wrist to his mouth and whispered something. He had either a small elf in there or a mic.

"Sir, I'm going to need to ask you to come with

me," he said, this time making it clear it wasn't a question.

"Because I just rode a hot streak at one of your tables?"

"I just have a couple of questions for you."

I was irritated. I wasn't sure what I had done, other than win more than I'd ever won at a blackjack table. I'd tipped the dealer well. I wasn't drunk. I was being hassled.

"Then you can ask them right here or cash in my chips," I said. "Or I'm about to get very loud and obnoxious."

"I'd advise against that."

I looked at Doreen. "I'd like my money, please."

She didn't move.

I looked back at the suit. "What the hell is going on?"

"Just some routine questions, sir."

"About?"

"It won't take long."

I collected my chips and stuffed them in my pockets. "It won't take long, because it's not going to happen."

He lifted his arm and spoke into his wrist again.

I pushed past him and headed for the elevators. He stayed right on my heels, still talking to his wrist.

Out of the corner of my eye, I saw two more suits approaching. I quickened my pace to the elevators. I got to the bank of lifts and punched the UP button.

"I'm a guest here in the hotel," I said. "I'm going up to my room."

"No, sir," the first suit said. "You aren't. We need you to come with us."

"I've done nothing wrong," I said, unsure of why I was feeling so defensive.

"I didn't say you did, sir."

One of the elevators dinged, and I stepped toward it.

The suit put his hand on my shoulder, and the two others stepped in closer. I pushed his hand off of my shoulder and squared off with him.

The other two were quick to take me to the floor, and I went down flat on my chest, my chips spraying into the air and landing all around me.

The elevator doors opened, and I managed to twist my head to look up. Julianne stepped out, her hair still damp from her shower.

She looked at the suits, then down at me.

She folded her arms across her body. "This isn't helping my stress level."

22

"Don't I get a phone call?" I asked.

I was sitting at a marble table in the middle of a sparsely decorated office. The suits were standing near the door, looking at me with bored expressions. One of them had gathered my spilled chips and stacked them neatly on the table. I had no idea where Julianne was.

"You aren't under arrest," said the original suit.

"Feels like it."

"Sorry you feel that way. As I said out there—before you caused a commotion—we just had a few questions for you."

"So ask them, now that you're detaining me in here."

"You aren't being detained."

"So I can go?"

"Very soon."

I pointed at the door behind them. "My wife is an attorney. I guarantee you she's out there, about to sue the crap out of this place."

"Perhaps."

I sighed and leaned back in the chair. I still had no idea what I'd done other than win a bunch of money. I'd never experienced a winning streak like that before, but I doubted this was normal protocol.

As I continued to wonder what was going on, there was a sharp knock on the door and the suits quickly stepped to the side. The door opened.

A woman about my age with long blond hair, a pointed chin, and thick black glasses walked in. She wore a navy blue business suit and a stern expression. She held a sheet of paper, reading it closely.

She glanced at the suits. "Thank you, gentlemen."

They quickly filed out.

She laid the paper on the table and extended her hand. "Mr. Winters, I'm Myrtle Callaghan, director of security here at Comanche River."

I did not shake her hand. "Good for you."

She retracted the hand, unoffended, and sat down in the chair at the head of the table. "I apologize for interrupting your evening."

"You did more than that."

"When a patron enjoys a tremendous run of luck like you experienced, we generally send an employee over to make sure everything is on the up-and-up," she explained. "Does that make sense?"

My inclination was to tell her where to shove her tremendous run of luck, but I could hear Julianne's voice in my head.

"I have no intention of having a conversation with you," I said. "Your employees harassed me, and I've done nothing wrong. I think I'll wait until my attorney gets here."

"To be clear, you aren't here because you won, Mr. Winters," Myrtle Callaghan said. "You won fair and square, and I congratulate you." She motioned to the chips on the table. "That is your money, and you'll be allowed to take all of it with you when we are finished here. And if you'd like to continue gambling, you are welcome to do that, as well."

"Then why the hell am I in here?"

Myrtle adjusted her glasses. "You asked a particular question of the dealer who was presiding over your game."

Now I started to feel a little self-conscious. I kept my mouth closed.

"About an employee with the last name Huber? Do you recall that?"

I squirmed in my seat. "Yes."

"Can you tell me why you were asking about an employee with that last name?"

"Not really."

"Not really, Mr. Winters?"

We sat there in silence for a moment, a clock on the wall ticking loudly.

Myrtle adjusted the glasses again. "Mr. Winters, we do, in fact, employ someone with that last name here at Comanche River. But, you see, there's a little problem."

"What's that?"

"Mr. Elliott Huber disappeared several days ago," she explained. "And it appears he may have taken some of the casino's money with him."

23

"Before I came in here," Myrtle Callaghan said, "I ran a quick background check on you. I saw that you are an investigator. I hoped you might be able to help us or, at the very least, share any information you might have."

"Why didn't you just tell me that out there?"

"I didn't want that discussion taking place out on the floor, in front of patrons and other employees. I'm sure you can understand that."

I could. It made sense. I still wished they would've been up front about their reasons rather than going all secret agent on me, but I understood what she was saying.

"I don't know much," I said and then told her what I knew.

She nodded when I was finished. "Yes, the cousin is of interest to us, too. He was here. Frequently."

"Gambling?"

"At times. Another time he applied for a job. But most of the time, it seems as if he came to meet with his cousin."

"Any idea why?"

She shook her head. "None. But he was here the day before the money disappeared."

"How did it disappear?"

She shifted in her chair, uncomfortable. "I really can't share that information at this juncture."

"Why not?"

"It doesn't reflect well on the casino and our procedures. We'd prefer to keep it quiet."

I nodded. "Okay. Can I ask how much money you believe he stole?"

She pursed her lips, thinking hard over the question for a moment. "Fifty-seven thousand dollars, give or take. Given the whole scheme of the business we do here, it's a very insubstantial sum. But it's still fifty-seven thousand dollars."

"I understand. And you've heard nothing from him?"

"Nothing. And we've been . . . diligent in our attempts to locate him."

I imagined the suits being very diligent in their attempts to locate him. They'd probably gone easy on me, and I hadn't stolen any money.

Myrtle Callaghan stood and produced a business card. "If you learn anything, I'd appreciate a phone call. As quickly as possible."

I fished into my wallet and handed her a card. "Same here."

She looked at the card, then nodded. "Certainly. Again, I apologize for the inconvenience and interruption of your evening. We're going to upgrade you to a suite for the evening for your trouble. Just let me know when you and your wife are ready to return to your room and I'll have our staff move your belongings. I think you'll be pleased with the new accommodations."

She stepped to the door and opened it. "Mrs. Winters?"

Julianne stepped into the doorway.

"We're all finished," Myrtle said. "I just explained to your husband that we'll be upgrading your accommodations for the evening. I'll let him give you the details. My apologies again for the inconvenience."

Julianne nodded, and Myrtle Callaghan disappeared out into the hallway, closing the door behind her.

Julianne's lips were pressed together tightly, and her arms were still folded across her chest.

"When the pizza showed and you didn't," she said, "I figured you were sitting at a table. Or a slot machine. Not playing detective."

"That's not what I was doing, Jules."

"Really?"

"Well, no. I mean, yes. I mean, no. Wait."

"I thought we came up here for some me and you time."

"We did."

"Then I find out you're down in the casino, hassling some dealer about the King of Soccer."

"I wasn't hassling her."

"And I certainly didn't expect to find you being tackled by a bunch of security people."

"That wasn't my fault."

"Of course not. Maybe you tripped and they fell on you."

"Jules, come on."

She poked a thumb over her shoulder. "What did Hot Security Director mean about new accommodations?"

"They're upgrading us. To a suite. Because I didn't do anything wrong."

She chewed on her lip for a moment, then nodded. "Okay, here's how the rest of the evening is going to go. We're going to go upstairs and eat, because I'm starving. Then we are going to have boring, uneventful sex, because while I still want a baby, I don't want to give you the pleasure of having super sexy me. Because you have totally screwed up our night."

I felt my shoulders sagging.

"So I'm going to lie on my back, and you are going to deposit your sperm in me," she continued. "There will be no pleasure involved. Think of it as a business transaction. It's the least you can do. And this suite . . . how big is it?"

"I have no idea, but she said we'd be pleased."

She turned and opened the door. "Excellent. That means it should be nice and big and roomy. With lots of furniture."

I stood, thinking she was softening. "Exactly."

She looked back over her shoulder. "So at least you'll be able to sleep on a sofa rather than the floor after we've had boring, uneventful sex."

24

I woke up with a knot in my back.

The suite had turned out to be the largest at Comanche River but was furnished with mostly easy chairs rather than sofas. I'd crammed myself into a love seat after having cold, awkward sex with Julianne and spent the night tossing and turning, trying to get comfortable. I kept thinking she might come out and invite me to bed, but I should've known better.

I sat up and stretched out my legs, trying to unkink my lower back without much luck. I stood and bent over and touched my toes, loosening the muscles as much as I could.

"I'd bow to me, too, if I'd been an idiot last night," Julianne said.

I stood up. "Good morning."

She was standing there in an A&M T-shirt and old cotton shorts, holding two coffee mugs. "Back hurt?"

"Yes."

"Good." She walked over, handed me a mug, and

sat down on the love seat, tucking one leg beneath her. "I love you, Deuce."

"I love you."

"But you drive me nuts sometimes."

I sat next to her. "I know."

She sipped from the mug. "And let's not beat around the bush here, okay? You are not the best at this. Not for lack of trying, but you are not the best."

"I know."

"Stop being so agreeable."

"Okay."

She rolled her eyes, but I wasn't sure what she wanted me to say.

"So my feelings are a little hurt," she said.

"I'm sorry."

"I know you are, but my feelings are crying. Sobbing, really. You brought me up here under false pretenses, and now I feel like a third wheel."

"That doesn't even make sense."

"Oh, it does to me, and, really, you should just be agreeing with me."

"You just told me to stop being so agreeable."

"Well, I am allowed to be confusing since you've made me feel like a third wheel."

"Jules."

She cracked a tiny smile. "So you need to make it up to me."

"How?"

"Well, I'm not pregnant yet."

I raised an eyebrow. "How do you know?"

"A woman always knows."

"You brought a test with you, didn't you?"

"Three. In case I needed reassurance."

I laughed. That sounded exactly right.

"So what are you suggesting?" I asked.

"You know how last night I sort of punished you by having boring, lame sex with you?"

"I remember. Vividly."

"Let's do exactly the opposite."

And that was what we did for the next hour, as I tried to make up for my complete jackassery the night before.

To Julianne's credit, she forgives. She doesn't hold grudges. At least against me, she doesn't. She can go off like a teapot left on the stove for too long, but after the steam has blown off and evaporates, she's willing to let bygones be bygones. I'm not sure if that's a product of her personality or a necessity in being married to me. Maybe a little of both.

We enjoyed the rest of the morning in the hotel suite, and then we headed down to the casino floor to spend my winnings from the previous evening. We ended up dumping most of it back into the casino, as my luck was the complete opposite. I couldn't win a hand to save my life, and I clearly infected Julianne, as she couldn't win a dime on any slot she pulled. But we had fun doing it, and when we checked out, my idiocy seemed to be in the rearview window.

The car was low on gas, so I crossed the highway when we left the casino parking lot, and pulled into a giant truck stop–slash–gas station to fill up the van. Julianne ran inside to grab a couple of bottles of water, and that was when I noticed the guy watching me.

He was in an orange VW Bug, not the most inconspicuous car to follow someone in, parked off to the side near the main part of the truck stop. I had seen the car pull out of the casino lot behind us and hadn't thought anything of it. But when I saw the car parked near the store and then the guy's eyes follow Julianne in and then revert back to me, it seemed pretty clear that he was watching me.

I fiddled with the gas pump, staring at him from behind my sunglasses. He had on a baseball cap over long hair, and he had a really long mustache. He was fidgeting. Something seemed amiss, but I couldn't place it from a distance.

Julianne came back out from the store with two bottles of water, crossed the lot, and slid back into the seat.

I leaned into my driver's side window. "Okay, I know I screwed up last night, but what would you think if I said I think someone is following us?"

She unscrewed the cap from one of the bottles. "I'd say I believe you."

"You would?"

She took a long drink from the bottle. "Yes. The orange Bug, right?"

"How'd you know?"

"I saw him follow us out of the casino and just thought he was a casino freak." She frowned. "I saw him parked over there when I went into the store."

"Maybe Victor and I should hire you."

"Maybe."

I glanced through the windows on the opposite side of the car. He was still sitting there, watching us.

"I'm going to go talk to him," I said.

"What should I do?" Julianne asked. "Provide backup?"

"No. Just sit here and look beautiful."

"You've already apologized. There's no need to resort to flattery."

"Well, it's for next time. Like a down payment."

"Hmmm. I'm not sure I take deposits."

"I'll be right back."

I unhooked the nozzle from the car and set it back on the pump. I closed the gas cap, paused for a moment, and then headed toward the Bug.

He sat up straighter as I approached, but made no move to turn on the car or get out. He tugged on the bill of the baseball cap but, other than that, seemed unfazed by my approach.

I held up a hand. "Hi there."

His window was down. He looked the other way first, then turned back to me. "Hey."

"Can I help you?"

He looked the other way again, then came back to me. "We hope so."

"We?"

"You're Winters, right?"

"Yeah. Who are you?"

He fingered the mustache. It moved awkwardly, and I realized it was a fake. "Someone who needs your help."

"Uh, okay."

He glanced around nervously, then pulled on the bill of his cap again. All of his hair moved at the same time. The wig was a fake, too.

"My cousin and I," he said, "we need your help."

"Wait. You're Moises's cousin?"

He nodded, and half the mustache came loose. He pressed it back to his lip. "Yes. I'm Elliott."

"You work at the casino?"

"Yeah. Or I did, I guess." He glanced around

again. "Look, man, we can't talk here. They might be watching."

"They?"

"Yeah. Follow me and we can go talk."

"My wife's with me."

"Is she cool?"

"I think so, but she's my wife."

He thought hard for a moment. "Okay. Bring her along."

"Where are we going?"

"Just follow me. But not too close. I need to keep my eyes open for anyone else who might be close behind."

"Okay."

He started the Bug and pulled away. He waited at the end of the line of pumps.

I walked back to the car and slid into the driver's seat. I looked at Julianne. "Feel like going for a drive?"

25

We followed Elliott Huber out of the gas station and along the frontage road of the highway for about ten minutes before we turned off and cut down a country road that seemed to lead absolutely nowhere. But after a few miles, barns and farmhouses began dotting the countryside and signs of civilization reappeared.

"Is this a good idea?" Julianne asked, staring out the window. "Following some weird guy into the country?"

"Probably not."

"Okay. Just asking."

I had tried to call Victor but got his voice mail, so I'd left him a message about where we were and what we were doing. He hadn't called back.

"How did he find you?" Julianne asked.

"No clue," I said. "He didn't say."

"You might wanna ask him that."

"Duly noted. I was a bit distracted by all the fake hair."

"I can't wait to see it up close."

"The wig is better than the mustache."

"I'll be the judge of that."

We turned off of the country road we'd been traveling on, and the wheels of the minivan crunched the gravel on a road that wound up and over gently rolling hills. At the bottom of the hills were two buildings, a small farmhouse and a large barn.

The Bug parked next to the barn, and we pulled in next to it.

Elliott got out and stood next to his car, watching me carefully. Julianne came around to my side of the car.

"This is my wife," I said. "Julianne."

She held up a hand. "Hello."

He nodded but didn't say anything. He readjusted the hat again.

"The mustache is pretty good," Julianne whispered.

Elliott seemed to be deliberating on something, but I wasn't sure what.

"Now what?" I asked. "You asked me to follow you, and I did."

He walked to the barn. "Wait here."

He pried open the large doors and disappeared inside, closing the doors behind him.

"Well, this seems totally normal," Julianne said, leaning back against the van.

"We can leave," I offered. "We don't have to stay."

"Maybe the barn is filled with fake hair products."

"That would be creepy."

"But fun."

"If you say so."

"Do you think the soccer guy is in there?" Julianne asked, glancing at the barn.

"I'm guessing yes."

"What if he's not?"

"Then we will be getting back in the van and heading home."

"You are so sexy when you have a plan."

"Thank you."

The barn doors opened, and Elliott emerged.

He walked over to us. "What are you going to do with Moises if you find him?"

"You mean when I walk into the barn and find him?"

"No. He might not be in there. I mean when you find him."

I shuffled my feet against the gravel. "I want to ask him some questions about some missing money. And trophies."

"Are you going to arrest him?"

"I'm not a cop."

"You aren't?"

Elliott was wearing on my patience. "No. I'm not. I thought you knew who I was."

His mouth twisted. "I do. I mean, I think I do."

"Your cousin knows me."

"Not well."

"But he knows I'm not a cop."

"Maybe you're undercover," Elliott said, his eyes narrowing. "Maybe you're wearing a wire."

I turned to Julianne. "Let's go. We are wasting our day here."

"Wait!" Elliott cried. "Don't go!"

"Then tell me why we are here, or we are leaving," I said, irritated.

"My cousin is in the barn. He is not elsewhere."

"I know."

"How did you know?"

I couldn't understand how anyone this dense had managed to steal money from a casino.

"I was just guessing," I said.

Elliott nodded slowly. "Good guess. I guess you are a good detective."

I glanced at Julianne. "See? I'm good at my job."

She raised an eyebrow. "*This* is your evidence?"

She had a point.

"Come on," Elliott said, motioning to the barn. "My cousin wants to speak with you."

About time.

26

The inside of the barn was massive and warm, filled with haystacks and old farming tools. Rays of sunlight fought their way in through the cracks in the exterior.

Elliott walked us over to a computer on top of a blanket on top of a haystack.

"Where's your cousin?" I asked.

"He's not here."

"You told me he was."

"I was fooling you."

"See?" Julianne said. "I told you he wasn't a good reference."

"We're leaving," I said. "I don't like games, Elliott, and you've been goofing around since you were spying on us at the gas station."

"I actually started spying on you at the casino," he said.

"Whatever. We're leaving."

"You don't wanna speak to Moises?"

"He's not here. You said so yourself."

"But we can speak with him."

"How? Telepathy?"

"I don't know what that means," Elliott said.

I sighed. "How can we talk to Moises?"

"He's being held hostage."

"Hostage?"

"Yes, but he's all right."

"Do you know where he is?"

"No."

"Then how are we going to talk to him?"

He pointed at the silver laptop. "On that."

I looked at Julianne. She shrugged.

"I can contact him," Elliott said. "But I don't know where he is. His kidnappers are totally devious."

"You know who they are?"

The skin around his jaw tightened. "Yes. They are evil."

"Who are they?"

"I can't say. They might come after me."

He moved his eyes to the ground, staring at his feet.

His fear seemed real, so I left it alone for the moment.

"Okay," I said. "Let's talk to your cousin."

Elliott knelt at the laptop and booted it up.

"Where are we, by the way?" Julianne asked. "Whose farm is this?"

"I dunno," Elliott said. "The house is vacant. But I can still get Wi-Fi out here."

"How did you find it?" she asked.

"I was just driving," he said. "I didn't want to be near the casino."

"Which reminds me," I said. "Did you take the money from the casino?"

"Let's talk to Moises first," he said. "Then it will make sense."

I doubted that but said nothing.

He logged into Skype, pushed the call button, and waited. The Skype application rang, but there was no answer.

"Weird," Elliott muttered.

He disconnected the call and tried again.

The application dialed again, and the ring was interrupted almost immediately.

"I'm here. I'm here," a voice said. "Sorry. I was finishing lunch."

"I'm here with Deuce Winters," Elliott said.

"And his wife," Julianne said.

"And his wife," Elliott repeated. "I think they are okay."

Other than the headache I was getting.

"All right," Moises said.

The screen blinked, and Moises appeared on it. The shot was tight, mostly of his face. He hadn't shaven since I'd seen him last, but otherwise he looked fine. All I could make out in the background was a white headboard and some obscured photos on the wall. He appeared to be sitting in a bedroom, but I couldn't be sure.

He held up a hand. "Hi, Deuce."

"Hey, Moises. How are you?"

He appeared a bit confused as to how to answer that. "Uh, I'm all right, I guess."

"Okay."

"How are you?"

"Well, I'm confused as to what's actually going on here. Your cousin brought me here and tells me you're being held hostage or something, and now you're on the computer, and I don't really know anything more than I knew this morning."

Moises nodded. "Yeah, I could see that."

"So I'm really hoping I'm going to get some answers here."

"I took the money," he blurted out. "I had to."

"All right."

"I didn't have a choice."

"So someone made you?"

"Yes. I mean, no." He frowned. "Yes and no, I guess."

"You aren't making sense."

"I know."

"Start at the beginning."

Moises glanced to the side. "I don't have much time."

"So you took the money?"

He hesitated. "Yes. I'm sorry."

"Do you still have it?"

"No."

He was basically admitting a felony to me. I wasn't sure what to say to that.

"That's going to be a problem, Moises," I said. "I might be able to help if you were able to return it, but if you can't . . ."

"I know."

"I'm assuming you can't tell me where you are."

A black police baton entered the picture and hovered near his neck, a reminder that he couldn't say too much.

"No, I can't."

The baton retreated.

"I'm not exactly sure what you need from me,

Moises," I said. "I don't know that I'm in a position to help."

"I need more money."

"More?"

"Yes."

"Why?"

He glanced to the side. "I can't say."

I really wasn't sure why Moises Huber thought I might lend him money. We weren't close friends. We were acquaintances. Everything felt a little out of place right at that moment.

"I need to go," he said. "They say I need to go."

The screen went black, and the call was disconnected.

Elliott closed the laptop. "Well, there you have it."

"Elliott, no offense," I said, feeling the anger inside me about to erupt, "but I have *nothing*."

"What do you mean?" he asked, looking both confused and offended. "You spoke to my cousin."

"Yes. For a couple of minutes. And all he did was ask me for more money."

"Yes. Can you give it to him?"

"Absolutely not!" I said.

Julianne's hand touched my shoulder, her signal for me to tone it down and cool off.

I took a deep breath. "No. I won't give you or him or anyone any money."

Elliott's shoulders sagged, and he sat on a haystack. "They are going to hurt him. I know it."

I tried a different tack. "Your cousin admitted to taking the money. He says he needs more. Why would he need more?"

Elliott rubbed at his chin and then pulled off the

fake mustache. He wadded it up and threw it to the ground. "Because he owes more. We owe more."

"Owe? To who?"

"To them."

"Who's them?"

The fear I'd seen earlier returned to his face. "The girls."

27

"Look, I'm not talking about the girls. Not a chance," Elliott Huber said.

I had spent ten minutes trying to get him to open up about whoever was holding Moises hostage, but had had no luck in pulling any details from him. He was adamant in refusing to talk about whoever it was, and his fear seemed born out of actual experience rather than any sort of deception.

"Okay," Julianne said, sensing my frustration and giving me a second to regroup. "Let's talk about the money, then."

He pulled off the ball cap and the wig to expose a head of short, black, spiked hair. "Okay."

"Moises admitted that he took the money," I said. "Did you take yours from the casino?"

He nodded slowly. "Yeah."

"Why?"

"To help him."

"Why does he need so much money?"

Elliott's mouth twisted, and he fidgeted.

"I'm assuming it's gambling," I said.

He looked up at me. "Why do you say that?"

"Things I've heard. You work in a casino. Sorta fits."

He looked past me. "Yeah. It's gambling."

"So he needed the money to pay a debt?"

"Yeah."

"To these girls?"

"Man, I'm not saying anything about them."

"I'm going to assume it's them."

"Whatever."

"So he owes them money, and now they've kidnapped him or something because he hasn't paid them," I said, glancing at Julianne.

She shrugged, then nodded. She was as lost as I was.

"If you had to steal for him, his debt must be huge," I added.

"It is."

"So what do these girls want? Just their money?"

He shifted on the hay bale. "No."

"What else?"

"I'm not supposed to say."

I looked at Julianne. "I can't believe we've wasted an entire Saturday with this ridiculousness. I'm sorry."

"It's okay," she said. "Let's go."

I grabbed her hand and we headed for the barn doors.

"Wait. You're leaving?" Elliott asked.

"Yes. We're leaving. I'm going to go home and try to salvage this day."

"I thought you were going to help us."

"And I thought you weren't going to jerk me around," I said. "But that's all you've done. And it's gotten old. So we're gonna go home and pick up our daughter and do something a little more rewarding than sitting around with some jackass in a fake mustache and fake wig who talks in circles."

He flinched, like a pet who'd been scolded. "I'm sorry."

We reached the barn doors. "Me, too."

"It's the trophies," he said. "They want the trophies."

"The soccer trophies?" I asked.

"Yeah. But I don't know why. I swear."

"So they want to exchange him for the trophies?"

"And the money I took," he said.

My head spun. None of it made any sense.

"Where are the trophies?" I asked.

"I don't know."

"Why do they want them?"

"I don't know. I swear."

"You should just call the police, Elliott," I said. "I don't think I can help you."

"Moises said not to."

"Well, Moises has sorta gotten you into a lot of trouble, hasn't he? Maybe you need to stop listening to him."

"Can you at least help me find the trophies?" he asked. "Please?"

I opened the door for Julianne. "Remind me to tell Victor to fire me when we get home."

28

I was exhausted by the time we got home, worn out by the shenanigans and the utter waste of time brought on by the cousins Huber. Julianne was polite enough to take Elliott's phone number as we left the barn, but at that moment, I had no intent on using it.

We picked up Carly at my parents' house and took her home, aiming for a quiet afternoon and evening with our daughter. She was happy to be home with us, but tired, as she usually was after a night or two with her grandparents. She put her head down on the living room floor as the three of us played Candy Land and was asleep in about thirty seconds.

"Do we just let her nap there?" Julianne asked.

"She'll wake up if we move her."

"Okay."

I pushed the game board to the side and scooted next to her as Carly started to snore on the floor.

"I'm sorry the weekend went to crap," I said.

"Weekend is only half over," she said. "And I owe you an apology, too."

"Why's that?"

She took a deep breath and sighed. "Because I have been a royal bitch about having a baby."

"No, you haven't."

She held up a hand. "Yes, I have. Don't argue. I know when I'm being me and when I'm being a pain in the ass, and that is all I have been for the past few days."

"Okay."

She grabbed my hand and squeezed it. "You may not know this about me, but I'm a little obsessive."

"You don't say."

She smiled. "Exactly. So I know I'm caught up in this baby thing. I'm just a little . . . anxious."

"Why?"

She pursed her lips and dipped her chin. She blinked several times, staring into her lap.

"I really want her to have a sister or brother," she said. "But what if it doesn't happen?"

Something snagged in my gut. "Why wouldn't it happen? Is something wrong?"

She squeezed my hand, moved her eyes to me. "No. Nothing is wrong. At all. I promise."

I let out a long breath. "Okay."

"I just worry about what it would be like if we couldn't have another," she said. "Would she be lonely? Would we feel unsatisfied? I don't know. It's just this . . . thing . . . on my mind right now. And I can't shake it and it's silly and it's turned me into a bit of a lunatic."

I let go of her hand and put my arm around her shoulders. I didn't like seeing her worried, but it was nice to see a sign of vulnerability from her once in a while. She always seemed to have such a handle on everything in her life that I rarely saw her doubt anything that was going on.

"If for some reason we weren't able to have another baby, we would be fine," I said. "All of us. Her, you, and me. Fine. We'd find another way to fill the void. Adopt or something. I don't know. It's not silly at all, though. You want a baby. And you aren't exactly the most patient person walking the planet."

She laughed softly and laid her head on my shoulder. "Really?"

"Really. And that's okay, too. But we can't force it. It'll happen when it's time. And, yeah, that sounds awfully touchy-feely, but I'm not sure how else to put it." I kissed the top of her head. "And for the record, I really want another one, too. It's not just you. I just didn't make charts and graphs."

She slapped my thigh, and I laughed.

"I'm just feeling these motherly instincts," she said. "And I need to feed them. I want to nurture and care and change diapers and get up in the middle of the night. Again."

"Maybe we could rent a baby."

"No. I want full ownership."

"Ah. Okay."

She stood and pulled me up with her.

"Come upstairs with me," she whispered in my ear.

"Do we have the green light?"

She smiled and pulled on my hand. "I don't know and I don't care."

29

I woke to a midget poking me in the cheek.

"Get up, pretty boy," Victor said.

I rolled over, disoriented. The last I knew, Julianne was in bed next to me and we were sweaty and breathing heavy.

"Your gorgeous wife said to come wake you up," Victor said. "Said you were napping."

"You're like waking up to a real-life nightmare."

"Want me to hop in bed with you?" he asked. "Maybe spoon with you?"

"Jesus, no," I said, searching under the covers for my shorts. I pulled them on and threw the sheets off. "Move, or I'll step on you."

He chuckled and moved from the side of the bed. I found my T-shirt on the floor and pulled it on over my head. "What do you want?"

"Wanted an update," he said, hopping up into the old easy chair in the corner of the room. "On our case."

"I'm not sure it's our case anymore," I said and told him about our evening, morning, and afternoon.

"Well, that dude called me," he said when I finished.

"What dude?"

"The cousin."

"Elliott?"

"Yep. Says he'll pay."

"With what money?" I asked. "Thought he was stealing money to give to his cousin."

"Well, I didn't know that when he called," Victor said. "He just told me that he'd met with you today and that you weren't sure you wanted to help."

"I think he left out some details."

"Guess so. But if he's got money, I say yes."

"Isn't that some sort of conflict of interest since we're already helping Belinda?"

Victor shrugged his tiny shoulders. "I don't think so. The broad, we're helping her find the money. With this dude, we're looking for his brother."

"They're one and the same."

Victor rolled his eyes. "Look, we got two people willing to pay for our services. Rule number one for private investigators is always say yes to the money."

I made a face. My enthusiasm for investigating was fading. I wasn't involved this time, and I was tired of dealing with people who seemed to be missing a few screws. I didn't need the work. And I sure as hell didn't need the frustration.

"He said he'd meet with us Monday," Victor said, sensing my reluctance. "On our terms, wherever we wanted."

"He wouldn't tell me anything."

"We'll tell him it's one and done. Either he spills what he knows or we dump him and he can go find his own brother. Simple."

I doubted it was going to be simple, but I wasn't sure what else to say. "Fine."

He hopped down out of the chair. "Excellent. Monday morning for breakfast. I'll set it up." He stopped. "Hey. The swaddling thing? It worked."

"I told you it would."

"Well, you don't need to get all puffy about it. I'm just telling you it worked for us. He's sleeping and not crying so much."

"I told you it would."

His face screwed up in agitation. "I'm trying to say thank you, you big moron."

I smiled. "I know. I just wanted to hear you say it. And you're welcome. Let me know if you need help with anything else."

He made a face. "I won't need any other help from you. Guaranteed. I got this daddy thing wired."

"Sure you do."

"Go ahead, doubt me," he said, walking to the door. "But I got it down. Maybe I'll quit my job and sponge off my wife like you do. Play Daddy all day long and eat bonbons."

"Your wife probably puts the bonbons up high in the fridge," I said. "You'd have trouble reaching them."

"Your short jokes get old, moron," he said, sneering. "I've heard them all."

"Really? That sounds like a challenge."

"Bring it. I can handle you."

I lunged at him, like I was going to grab him. He jumped, spun, and sprinted out of the bedroom.

Both of my girls were awake when I went downstairs, and Julianne seemed very pleased with herself that she'd sent Victor to wake me up.

"That little man is funny," Carly said, working hard on a drawing of what was either a cow or a spaceship.

"If you say so," I said.

"Plus, he's my size."

"That is accurate."

We spent the rest of the evening eating dinner, playing games, and watching a little television. On Sunday we stayed close to home, playing out in the yard, picking up the house, and generally being lazy. By the time Monday morning rolled around, I felt back in sync with my life.

I dropped Carly at VBS and headed into town for my breakfast meeting with Victor and Elliott. I was still hesitant about working with Elliott, but at least I'd have Victor's opinion this time. As much as I hated to give him any credit, he knew his job and he did it well. If he thought we could work something out with Elliott, we probably could. What he lacked in social graces, Victor more than made up for in savvy business skills.

I found the two of them at a table near the front window of the diner on Main. Victor raised a small hand at me when I entered, while Elliott just stared blankly at me.

I took the seat next to Victor. "Morning."

"Morning," Victor said, holding a coffee mug with both hands.

Elliott nodded.

"I've just been getting to know Mr. Huber here," Victor said.

"Ah, lucky you."

Victor frowned at me. "Easy."

I looked at Elliott. "Just so we're clear, when Victor told me you contacted him, I was against working with you."

"Thanks for the info," he said.

"I gave you plenty of time to tell me what you knew and to come up with an idea of how to help you," I said, "but you wasted my day."

A waitress came, and I ordered pancakes, bacon, and coffee. Victor ordered the same. Elliott shook his head and sipped from his ice water.

"You have to understand," Elliott said, "I'm not exactly sure what I'm doing here."

"Well, that makes two of us," I said.

He set the water down. "I don't want to go to jail."

"You stole. From a casino," I said. "You aren't going to have much choice."

"We'll see," he said. "But forget about me. I wish to help my cousin."

"How much is he in for?" Victor asked.

"A little over a hundred thousand," Elliott responded.

"Then he's got enough to pay it off," I said.

Elliott looked at me, confused. "I don't think so."

"He took seventy-five thousand from the soccer association," I said. "And he stole a boatload more from the church. I don't even get now why you had to steal from the casino."

Elliott squinted at me. "Wait. Church? What?"

I recounted my conversation at the church with Haygood.

Elliott's expression hardened. "That is not true."

"What isn't?" Victor asked.

"Moises did not steal that money."

"How do you know?" I asked.

His eyes shifted away from us for a moment. "I would know if he did that."

"Maybe he owed more than you knew about," Victor said.

Elliott shook his head. "No. Not possible."

I looked at Victor and shrugged. "Just telling you what I was told."

"He had a gambling problem?" Victor asked. "You don't deny that, right?"

Elliott thought hard for a moment, then nodded. "Yes. He does."

"So isn't it possible that he might've been in deeper than he told you?" Victor asked.

Elliott tapped his fingers on the table. "It's possible, yes. But I don't think so."

"Why?" I asked. "Why are you so sure?"

"Because he would've told me," he said. "And because he was doing other things to pay off his debts."

Victor raised an eyebrow. "Like?"

"I don't wanna say."

"Told you," I said, shaking my head.

Our food arrived, and I dug into it, thinking about what I was going to do with the rest of my day, because it sure didn't look like I was going to be doing anything to help Elliott Huber. Wash the car. I hadn't washed the car in forever, and it was going to be nice. . . .

"Look, pal," Victor said, shoveling pancakes into his mouth, "if you want our help, you're going to have to be an open book. End of story. Either you are or you aren't. It's pretty simple. And if you don't want to be, that's cool. Let's part friends now." He wiped his mouth. "Because if we agree to help and you hold out on us, I guarantee you, we will not part friends."

Like I said, Victor was good at his job. He managed to sum up everything I had tried to convey to Elliott in the barn in about ten seconds. He was a pain in the ass, but he was good.

Elliott leaned back in his chair, contemplating his next move.

We ate and drank coffee and said nothing.

"All right," Elliott said finally. "I understand. I will be an open book. But I need something else, then."

"We can't keep you out of jail," Victor said. "That isn't going to be our choice. Ultimately, you and the casino are going to have to work that out between yourselves."

Elliott shook his head vehemently. "That's not what I mean."

"What do you want, then?" I asked.

"Protection."

"Protection?" I glanced at Victor. "Like bodyguards?"

Elliott nodded. "Yes. I am going to need protection."

"We can't guarantee that, either," Victor said. "We can offer some suggestions, but we aren't bodyguards, pal."

Elliott thought that over. "These suggestions . . . they will help keep me safe?"

Victor shrugged. "Probably. If you're talking about hiding or whatever, I can help you with that. But not from the law."

Elliott's face tightened in anger. "I told you, I understand the legalities. I am not going to hide from the police once this is settled."

"So who are you going to hide from?" I asked. "Who do you need protection from?"

He fixed me with a hard stare. "The girls."

31

"You mentioned these girls the other day," I said after our plates had been cleared and our coffee cups had been refilled. "Who exactly are they?"

Elliott leaned into the table. "They are the ones who have Moises."

"You're sure?" Victor asked.

Elliott nodded. "I'm sure. They are evil, evil girls."

"Are they, like, his bookies or something?" I asked.

Elliott held a finger to his lips, indicating I was speaking too loudly. Then he nodded. "Yes. They are the ones who handle his bets."

"Who are they?" I asked.

"They are all young and pretty and act very nice," Elliott said, sneering, like he smelled something awful. "But you better believe they are nothing like that."

"Who are they?" I asked again.

Elliott set his jaw. "College girls."

I looked at Victor, and then we both burst out laughing. I wasn't sure what I expected to hear, but it certainly wasn't that. I couldn't even conjure up the image.

"I'm serious," Elliott said after our laughter died off. "Students. In a sorority at SMU."

I looked at Victor again, and we laughed even harder this time.

A look of annoyance took up residence on Elliott's face. "You don't believe me."

"What's the name of the sorority?" Victor asked. "We Takka Bets?"

I laughed and we high-fived.

Elliott's face reddened. "I am not making this up. They are the ones responsible for my cousin's gambling debt and the ones holding him hostage."

"I can think of much worse places to be held hostage," Victor said and then dissolved into a fit of giggles again.

Elliott looked at me. "The room he was in yesterday? What did it look like to you?"

I thought back to Moises's face on the computer screen. The white headboard. The baton.

"A girl's room," I said, glancing at Victor.

Elliott nodded. "Yes. Exactly. Because it was."

"Are you really trying to tell us he's being held against his will in a sorority house?" I asked.

Elliott sighed, irritated and frustrated. "Look, I don't know all the details, all right? But I do know that they are holding him against his will and that they are the ones he owes money to. You can believe me or not, but it's true. And the stories he's told me? These are not normal college girls." He shook his head. "Not normal at all."

Victor was still giggling, but I was starting to feel bad. Elliott was clearly telling us what he believed to be the truth. As absurd as it sounded, there was something there that made him believe it was fact.

"Do you know how Moises got hooked up with them?" I said. "How he started placing bets with them?"

Elliott shook his head. "No. I'm not sure how it started."

"What did he bet on?"

"Everything."

"Sports?"

"All sports. Even the kids' sports."

"Kids' sports?"

"The soccer program he is in charge of?" Elliott nodded. "He was betting on those games."

I felt like my head was going to explode.

"He was betting on kids' soccer games?" I asked, making sure I heard him correctly.

"Yes. He thought he could make a fortune on them since he ran the league and knew all the coaches and players and teams. But turns out it was hard."

No kidding. I thought of all the different things that affected Carly's team. Lack of sleep. Appetite. The weather. Planes overhead. There was no possible way to find any consistency in little kids. Betting on those games seemed like suicide.

And who in their right mind *took* bets on those games? Who set the lines?

"The sorority," Elliott said, reading my mind. "They set it all up."

I looked at Victor. "I don't even know what to say."

Victor just shook his head, unsure what to think.

"And there is something else," Elliott said.

"Of course there is," Victor said.

Elliott focused on me now that I seemed to be the one who was trying to take him seriously.

"When Moises's debt started to grow and it became obvious he couldn't pay it," Elliott said, "they asked him to start doing things."

"Doing things?" I asked.

"Illegal things."

I let out a long, deep breath. "All right. What kind of illegal things?"

Elliott again leaned into the table. "Smuggling."

"I think I've officially heard it all now," Victor muttered. "Really."

Elliott set his eyes on me. "You asked me about the trophies yesterday. You remember?"

"I remember."

"Those are what he is using now to smuggle."

"The trophies?"

Elliott nodded.

"What trophies?" Victor asked. "I'm lost."

I quickly explained the missing soccer trophies to him.

"These girls," Elliott said, "they are serious business. They are organized, and they know what they are doing. I think they finally just decided that they no longer trusted my cousin, and decided to hold him until he paid what he owed them." He shook his head. "And you can laugh all you want, but they are capable of many bad things."

I was trying to take him seriously. The things he was talking about—gambling, smuggling, kidnapping— were the things you tied to organized crime or gangs. It was difficult to place the faces of a sorority on those things.

But there was something sincere in Elliott now

that I had either missed or ignored the previous day. I wasn't sure he had all his facts right, but I believed that he thought he was telling the truth.

"They will hurt me if they know I'm talking to you," Elliott said. "I know this."

I nodded. "Okay. All right. We'll see if we can protect you."

"Wait, wait, wait," Victor said. "I wanna hear more about these trophies."

"I don't know all the details," Elliott said. "This was the first time he had to do that."

"So what was he doing with them?" I asked.

"He was hiding the stuff in the trophies," Elliott said. "I'm not sure what the plan was from there, but he had to fill up the trophies."

"Fill up?" I asked.

"The girls," he said. "With stuff that they sell."

"Drugs?" Victor asked.

"Yes, I suppose that's what you'd call it."

"You suppose?" Victor said. "They are either drugs or they ain't, pal."

"Yes, it was drugs," Elliott said. "But not what you are thinking. You are thinking cocaine or marijuana or something like that, right?"

Victor and I both nodded.

"Not those kinds of drugs," Elliott said.

"What kind then?" I asked.

Elliott leaned into the table. "Viagra."

32

"I don't know what they do with it," Elliott said as we walked out of the diner. "But that's what he had to pick up."

"Where?" I asked.

"He had to go down to Mexico," Elliott said. "He filled the trophies with the pills."

"Did you go with him?" Victor asked.

"No. He wouldn't let me."

"Do you know where the trophies are?" I asked. Elliott shook his head.

I looked at Victor. "I don't even know what to say."

"Me, either," Victor said. "Me, either."

"So you won't help us?" Elliott said.

"I didn't say that," I said, before I could stop the words from coming out of my mouth.

"We'll discuss it," Victor said, giving me a pointed look.

I ignored him. "You were able to contact Moises yesterday on Skype."

"Yes."

"Can you contact . . . the girls?" I asked.

He looked suddenly uncomfortable, like ants had made their way up his pants. "I don't know. Maybe."

"See if you can," I said. "I'd like to go meet with them."

"We'll discuss it," Victor growled.

"I'm not sure you want to do that," Elliott said. "I am not lying about them. My cousin has told me many stories."

"I'll take my chances," I told him.

"We'll discuss it," Victor yelled, tired of being ignored.

"After we discuss it," I said.

"I am unsure what to do now," Elliott said.

"Go home," I said.

"I'm not staying at home. For a lot of reasons. I'm at the barn."

"Then go back there. We'll be in touch later today. I promise."

He shook hands with each of us and walked down the block, disappearing around the corner.

"You can't honestly be serious," Victor immediately said.

"About?"

"About taking this nutcase on."

"Why is he a nutcase?"

His eyes bulged. "Hello? Did you not just hear his story?"

"I heard it."

"Then you have to know he's off his rocker."

"I don't think he is."

"So you think his cousin is being held captive by some rebel, machine gun–wielding college sorority?"

"He didn't say anything about guns."

"That was about the only thing he *didn't* mention."

"Right. So they aren't that bad."

"You're insane."

Maybe I was. I wasn't sure. Or maybe I just felt bad for the way I had treated Elliott the day before. Or maybe I was just curious. I didn't know. But I'd walked out of the diner wanting to help him.

"So don't help me," I said. "I'll take him on. You don't have to."

"Oh, please. You don't have a clue what you're doing, big boy."

"I'll figure it out."

Victor rolled his eyes. "Let's pretend for a second I let you do this. . . ."

"I don't need your permission."

"The heck you don't," he said, pointing a stubby finger at me. "We have a partnership."

He had me there. Our agreement was that we had to agree on what cases we took on. Neither of us had challenged that. Yet.

"So, let's say I let you have at this," Victor repeated. "You wanna know why I'm most concerned about this?"

"You'll miss the sale on jeans at the Children's Place?"

He sighed, not even bothering to get mad. "It's the casino."

"The casino?"

"That kook said he took the money from the casino. He admitted it."

"I know. I heard him."

"That ain't like stealing from some regular guy, Deuce," Victor said. "This is a whole 'nother thing."

I thought about my night at the casino, how quick they were to approach me, how quick they were to take me down. And how quick they were not to apologize for coming after me.

"Now, I'm not talking Vegas and mob men and all that," Victor said. "But they play by different rules. They will get their money back, one way or another. You don't steal money from casinos. You just don't."

"So maybe we can get the money back to them."

Victor squinted at me, like he'd never seen me before. "You think it's just sitting in a paper bag somewhere and you're gonna find it?"

"Maybe."

"You're more insane than that kook."

"Maybe."

"And what? When you find it, you're just gonna walk it back to the casino?"

"No. I'll drive."

"I'm not screwing around, Deuce."

I knew he wasn't, and I wasn't just blowing him off. But I felt like I'd already started the process of trying to help all these people in my life, and I didn't feel much like quitting on them just because it was getting a bit sticky. I wasn't disregarding Victor's ideas, but I wasn't ready to just bail on the whole thing.

"Let me poke around a little more," I said.

Victor frowned. "At least now you're asking me."

"Yes. I am. We're partners."

"Now you're just sucking up."

"Maybe. But let me do a little more work, and we'll see what turns up."

He stared at me for a moment, then threw his tiny hands up in the air. "Fine. But you got a short leash."

I started to say something, but he held up a hand.

"Yeah, I know what I just said," he said, stomping away. "Yuk, yuk, yuk, you big oaf."

33

I got back to my car, and my phone dinged immediately with a text. From Elliott.

Here is the number, it read, followed by a number. Just call it and leave a message. Don't tell them you got it from me, though. And be careful. I don't want my cousin to get hurt.

Elliott was truly afraid of these girls, or whoever they were. I knew I wasn't taking them seriously, and I wondered if I needed to change that attitude. But it was hard to think that someone's sorority rush chair might be so dangerous.

I called the number Elliott had texted me. A mechanical voice spoke to me over the line and told me to leave my name and number. No other information. I did as I was told.

My phone rang three minutes later, and I answered.

"Hi. This is Amber," a bubbly voice said. "Returning your call."

"Hi, Amber," I said, taken aback. I knew it was supposed to be a college girl, but it was off-putting to actually hear one. "I'm not exactly sure what the procedure is here."

"Hmmm. Well, tell me what you need."

"I'd like to . . . use your services."

She giggled. "That sounds mysterious!"

"Like I said, I'm new at this."

"Well, I appreciate, like, your honesty," she said. "The way that we do this normally is that we like to meet with you first. You know, just to get to, like, know you, okay?"

"That would be just fine. When and where?"

"You're eager! Awesome!"

"I try."

"Um, lemme see. I'm free in about an hour. How's that work?"

"Just fine. Where?"

She named a coffee shop near the university. I told her I could find it.

"And I won't be by myself, but you should be," she said. "Know what I mean?"

"Got it," I said. "I will be solo."

"Awesome! I'll be wearing a navy tank top and supercute denim shorts."

"I'm sure I'll be able to find you."

"See you soon!"

The phone clicked off.

I found it hard to believe that someone who wore supercute shorts was also running some sort of sophisticated gambling and smuggling ring and holding customers hostage until they paid their debts, but I didn't have anything else to go on. I was sure stranger things had happened, but at that moment, I couldn't think of any. I didn't really have a plan as to what I was going to do, so I was just planning on winging it.

SMU sits among the tony, old-money homes of North Dallas, with lots of ivy and red brick and white pillars. The school had lost its luster with the football scandal in the early eighties, but it was still viewed as a good regional school where lots of Dallas families were happy to send their kids and their money. The academics weren't terribly rigorous, but it was still looked upon as a better alternative than some of the state schools.

I found a parking spot on a crowded street filled with small restaurants, shops, and a used bookstore. The coffee shop was on the corner, and I spotted Amber at a table on the patio. She did, indeed, have on the aforementioned tank top and supercute shorts. Her long blond hair was pulled to the side in a ponytail; her eyes were hidden behind massive mirrored sunglasses. Her legs were crossed, the top leg bouncing as she typed away on her phone.

The girl next to her wore the same mirrored shades but noticed me about the same time I noticed them. Her dark hair was pulled back in the same way as Amber's, and there was more of it. She was chomping on gum. Her shorts were denim, but her tank top was red rather than navy. She set her pink rhinestone phone on the table and elbowed Amber as I walked to the table.

"Hi," I said. "Amber?"

She stuck out her hand and smiled at me. "Hey. Yep, I'm Amber."

We shook hands, and she pointed at the girl next to her. "This is Suzie."

Suzie waved at me but didn't smile.

"Sit, dude," Amber said.

I sat.

Amber upped the wattage in her smile. "So . . ."

"So . . ."

"How can we help?" Amber asked.

"Like I said on the phone, I'm not exactly sure what I'm doing here."

Suzie adjusted her glasses and chomped harder on the gum. "How'd you find us?"

"I'd rather not say."

"Well, like, I'd rather you do."

"Is that a make-or-break thing?" I said. "You need to know how I was referred or we can't . . . do anything?"

Suzie started to say something, but Amber placed a hand on her arm. "We're cool."

Suzie pursed her lips but didn't say anything.

"My friend just likes his privacy," I said.

"Totally cool," Amber said. "I get that."

"Great."

Amber glanced at Suzie and nodded. Suzie produced a sheet of paper and slid it across the table. I pulled it toward me and picked it up.

It was a tip sheet, as they call it in the gambling world. And nearly everything was on there. MLB, NFL, NBA, NASCAR. Whatever I wanted to bet on, it looked like they had it.

"Local on the other side," Suzie mumbled.

"Local?"

She made a flipping motion. I turned the tip sheet over.

And there it was. Teams from communities all around Dallas. I recognized the names of many of the soccer teams in our Rose Petal Youth Soccer Association. In fact, my Mighty, Fightin', Tiny Mermaids were favored by two in this Saturday's game.

It was all I could do not to scream, "What the hell?"

"Wow," I said. "That's interesting."

"Right?" Amber said with a big smile. "Now, a couple of things."

"All right."

"Are you a cop?"

"Nope."

Suzie leaned into the table. "You said that fast."

"It was an easy question."

"Still."

"I'm not a cop," I said, looking back to Amber. "Next?"

"Have you done this kind of thing before?" Amber asked.

"No."

"You'll need an account."

"An account?"

Suzie hesitated, then slid a card across the table to me. It listed a Web address.

"Go there," Amber said. "It'll walk you through the steps to put money in the account."

I thought about that for a moment. "Are there . . . minimums? Or maximums?"

Amber nodded. "Yes. They are on the site."

I reached a bit. "Because here's the deal. I've recently . . . come into a bit of money."

The girls exchanged glances, and Suzie chomped harder on her gum.

"It's play money, you know?" I said. "And I don't really wanna turn it over to the IRS in taxes, you know?"

Amber didn't acknowledge my comment, but Suzie nodded.

"So I'd just as soon . . . play with as much of it as possible. If you follow."

"Totes," Amber said.

"Totes?"

"Totally. I totally follow," she said seriously.

"Oh. Okay."

The two girls leaned closer together and exchanged whispers. They both nodded, satisfied.

"Let's stick to the rules right now," Amber said. "But then we'll see. We totally would love to help."

"Great. Can I ask a question?"

"Totes," Amber said, grinning.

I nodded at the tip sheet. "The local stuff. How do you go about setting those lines?"

"We've got a team," Suzie said.

"A team?"

Her mouth twitched, letting me know she was irritated with my questions. "We scout the games."

I raised an eyebrow. "I don't mean to be disrespectful, but you actually scout kids' soccer games?"

"And baseball and basketball," Amber said. "And football is huge. Huge."

"And people bet on those games?"

Amber leaned forward and dropped her sunglasses down her nose, exposing bright green eyes. "Dude, it's insane. Insane. Parents love to bet on their kids."

On one hand, it seemed crazy to me. Kids' sports were kids' sports. You signed your son or daughter up to give them something to do, to let them channel their energy into something. Yes, some parents harbored false hopes about the possibilities and took it too seriously, and it ended badly. But it was hard to imagine them using their kids as an avenue to money.

But the more I thought about it, the more it made sense. I could picture the angry faces, the loud mouths, the body language filled with tension of parents in the stands. I had always thought it was because they wanted their kids to do well and were a bit over competitive. If they had money on the line, though . . . maybe it made a little more sense.

I was just trying to wrap my head around it.

Suzie stood. "We need to roll."

Amber stood, too, and readjusted her sunglasses. "So we're good?"

I stood as well. "Yeah. We're good. I'm in. I'll get set up today."

"Sweet!" Amber squealed. "This is gonna be so much fun!"

Totes.

34

I dialed Elliott when I got back to my car. "I met with them."

"You didn't mention me, did you?"

"I didn't mention you or Moises."

He let out an audible sigh of relief. "Okay. What do you know?"

"Nothing."

"Nothing?"

I explained that I didn't want to give anything away until I got them to trust me and I saw how it all worked. I didn't want them to get scared off if I jumped on them about Moises right away.

"Hmmm," Elliott said. "I guess that makes sense."

"Does he have a time frame?" I asked. "Were there any sort of threats made about what they'd do to him if he didn't get them their money?"

"No. Not that he's told me."

"So you have your part of the money?"

"Yeah."

"Where is it?"

"I don't want to say."

Elliott still didn't trust me entirely, and I understood that.

"Okay. What about the trophies? Do you know where those are?"

"No. I'm trying to figure it out, but I honestly don't know."

"Would he tell you?"

He was quiet for a moment. "I don't know. I'm not sure he'd say in front of the girls, and they are always there when he's on the computer when I check in with him."

"Try to find out. Or at least think about where they might be."

"Okay. So this means you are going to help me?"

"Yeah, Elliott. I'm going to help you."

I expected him to thank me or sigh audibly again, but I picked up on something else.

"Elliott?"

"What is your fee?"

"We'll worry about it later."

"But I'm worrying about it now," he said. "I've given everything I have to my cousin. I have no money. And I'm probably going to prison. So . . . I don't know how I will pay you."

I wondered if any cousin I had would go to bat for me the way Elliott was for Moises. I didn't think they would. Despite all the weirdness, I liked Elliott.

"We'll work it out," I said. "After we help Moises."

"Your partner did not seem okay with that."

"I will handle him. Don't worry about it."

"You are much larger than him."

I smiled. "Yes. I am. I want you to do something for me, though."

"All right."

"Clarify with Moises exactly how much he owes."

"I already told you."

"I know. But clarify with him. Just to make sure."

"Okay," he said, confused. "I will do that."

I told him I'd be in touch, and we hung up.

I knew Elliott didn't understand why I wanted him to double-check on the money. That was fine. There were a lot of moving pieces to this case, and I was trying to keep them from getting away from me. The one thing that I still didn't have a handle on was the money.

I wasn't good at math, but nothing was adding up.

35

I picked up Carly at camp on Friday, and Julianne came home early so we could have an early dinner. It was the one night of the month where my responsibilities as dad and husband were suspended for an evening and I got to go play with the boys.

Dorky dad poker night.

I couldn't remember exactly how it had started, but several years back, someone suggested that we should get a poker game together. After several months of saying that sounded like a great idea, one of the dads on the soccer team finally arranged it, sent out the e-mails, and it began.

Now, one night a month, we gathered together to make fools of ourselves. We brought crappy food, beer and booze, and twenty bucks and played stupid card games until the wee hours of the morning. We made fun of one another, talked about our kids and wives and jobs, and exchanged a little money. It was a great way to forget about the daily grind and be giant goof-offs for a while once a month.

It was also a chance for them to give me grief about staying home and not working.

We rotated homes each month, and this month we were at Tom Shearer's. We all lived about ten minutes from one another, and more often than not, I'd walk to whoever's house we were playing at, just in case I had too much to drink and couldn't drive home. So I dropped my cookies and my giant bag of M&M's into my bag with my six-pack of Shiner and walked the six blocks over to his house.

As usual, I was the last one to arrive, and they enjoyed the fact that even though I wasn't rushing home from work, I still couldn't get there on time.

The regulars were there. Tom, Paul, Mark, Raphael, Jeff, Rich, and Brandon. We had others that might show up occasionally, but generally it was the eight of us. We considered ourselves dedicated, hardcore players.

Who regularly forgot all the rules to the games we made up.

I was five bucks down and two beers in when Paul nodded in my direction. "So . . . what's up with soccer?"

"We'll probably lose this week. The Red Hens are tough."

"Not what I mean. I mean with the association."

"What do you mean?"

Tom dealt. "He's being evasive."

"I'm not being evasive."

Tom nodded. "Yeah, you are."

"I mean, what's going on now that the association has no money?" Paul said.

I sighed and looked at my cards. They were awful, and I folded immediately when the bet came to me.

"I truly don't know," I said. "And that's not being evasive."

"That midget dude know anything?" Jeff asked, frowning at his cards.

"That guy freaks me out," Rich muttered behind his cards.

Raphael tossed a chip into the pot. "Midgets freak me out. Period."

"He's all right," I said. "I should invite him to this."

The room went silent.

"Kidding," I said.

"Midgets cheat," Brandon said.

"That's a fact," Mark said.

"Shut up and play," I said. "And I really don't know what's going to happen. I'm trying to fix it."

"What does that mean?" Mark asked.

"It means I'm looking for the money."

Paul shoved two chips to the middle of the table, and several of the guys groaned. "You still like the investigating gig?"

"It's fine, yeah."

"But it's not, like, a job, right?" Tom said, snickering.

"It's a job."

They all laughed and rolled their eyes.

"I'm benching all your kids this weekend," I promised. "All of them."

The night continued on like that, and I managed to hang even for a while, losing a little and winning a little. The best part of the game was that no one ever went home broke. Unless they did something really stupid and bet way over their head. There was no limit on the game, and we prided ourselves on letting each other do something absolutely ridiculous if we chose to do so.

I was down a little and full of M&M's and chicken wings when I threw it out there.

"You guys ever hear of betting on kids' games?" I asked.

Tom eyed his cards. "What kind of kids' games?"

"Soccer. Football. T-ball. Whatever."

"I bet Jeff his kid would cry before kickoff one time," Paul said.

"And you won," Jeff said, shaking his head.

We laughed.

"Not what I mean," I said. "I mean on the actual games."

"Think I bet one of the guys I work with one time," Brandon said. "Football game. We bet ice cream or something."

I shook my head. "No. I mean real betting."

They all made the kind of noises grown men make when they want to make another grown man feel stupid.

So it was like a third grade PE class.

After the noises and razzing settled down, Tom said "Yeah."

I looked at him. "Yeah, what?"

"Yeah, I've heard about it."

"You're full of crap," Paul said, perusing his cards.

Tom shook his head. "Nope."

"Tell me," I said.

He stared at his cards for a moment, then laid them flat on the table. "I'm out, anyway."

The others laid their cards down, listening.

"About a year ago," he explained, "guy at the

office asked who Emma's team was playing. I had no clue. I never know that crap."

They all nodded knowingly. They were nothing more than glorified chauffeurs to their families on the weekends. They went where their wives told them to go.

"So he pulls it up online, off the Web site or whatever," he continued. "Pulls up the records . . . You know how they post everyone's wins and losses and stuff?"

Everyone nodded again. They might not have known when the games were or who the opponents were, but they knew our win-loss record for every season we played. It was a man thing.

"And he says, 'I can get you good odds on your kid's team,'" Tom said matter-of-factly.

"Bull," Jeff said, frowning.

Tom shook his head. "Swear. I laughed, thought he was kidding. But then he punched in some Web site, and up it came. All the games, odds, payouts. It was all right there."

They murmured, exchanging looks of surprise and confusion.

"And you know me," Tom said, suddenly looking uncomfortable and shifting in his chair. "I bet on everything."

The rest of us were amateur gamblers at best, but Tom was the pro, if we had one. He traveled to Vegas, introduced new games, and rarely missed a monthly meeting. He knew how to gamble and how to bet, and he rarely went home in the red.

"You friggin' bet on the Mermaids?" Paul asked, his jaw hanging open.

"Three-to-one odds," Tom said, raising an eyebrow. "We were four and two at the time, facing a team that was oh and five."

They all grumbled for a moment, before they uttered what I knew was coming.

"The Anteaters game," they all said in unison.

Tom winced and nodded.

I remembered the game, too. The Anteaters were supposed to be one of those teams that everyone beat. They had new players every season, a new coach every season, and it usually added up to utter chaos. They rarely scored and rarely held teams under double digits.

But that fateful day everything aligned for them. Their kids came to play, and ours . . . did not. Girls were crying, didn't want to run, got hurt, basically forgot how to play soccer. I got so frustrated, I benched our starters and finished the game with our reserves. It was tantamount to throwing in the towel, and we lost four to three.

"We lost four to three," Tom said, right on cue. "Four to friggin' three."

"Because our *coach* decided to make a point," Paul said, his eyes narrowing in my direction.

"Hey. Your kid finished the game."

"His kid sucks," Rich said.

The others nodded in agreement.

"Exactly!" Paul cried. "She's awful. We had no chance when you put in my kid."

I rolled my eyes.

"And I lost a hundred bucks," Tom muttered.

All eyes moved to him.

"You bet a hundred bucks?" I said, incredulous. "On the Mermaids?"

"It was the Anteaters, for Christ's sake!" Tom said. "It was a sure thing!"

"I woulda made the coach pay," Raphael said. "Was his fault."

"Oh, shut up," I said.

"Three to one on our girls against the worst team known to man," Tom said. "Don't act like any of you wouldn't have done the same."

It was quiet.

"I would've bet more," Jeff finally said. "It was the friggin' Anteaters."

They all roared.

We settled into another game before I asked Tom another question.

"Did you place the bet, or did your coworker?" I asked.

"He did. You had to open up an account, and I wasn't comfortable doing that," Tom said. "I had to draw a line somewhere."

"*After* you bet on your kid's soccer game," Brandon reminded him.

"I gave him the money," Tom said, ignoring him. "He placed the bet. When we lost . . . or when *you* lost . . . the money was drafted out of his account in, like, half an hour." He shrugged. "It was all professional."

"Other than the preschool soccer part," Paul said.

"Other than that. But I promise you it was real, and I guarantee you if that site is still up and running, they are taking money on this weekend's games."

"You don't remember the Web site?" I asked.

Tom shook his head. "Nah. He wouldn't let me see it. He was protective of it. He wasn't supposed to let anyone else use it." He raised an eyebrow. "And he said that whoever ran the thing meant business. He wanted no part of messing with them. So he always had money in his account and always followed the rules."

That sounded familiar.

"From the way he talked, there were lots of other dads doing it," Tom said. "It almost seemed . . . normal."

So there was my answer. It was happening around me, and I didn't even know it. Sometimes, even though Rose Petal was small, it felt like I didn't know a thing about it. And if it was going on in Rose Petal, chances were it was happening everywhere. Who knew how extensive the operation was?

Well, Amber and Suzie probably did.

"When you pulled the starters that day," Tom said, shaking his head, "I nearly came over and strangled you."

"Sorry," I said. "You should've said something."

He burst out laughing. "Don't blow this. I've got a hundy on it."

"Yes. Absolutely."

"Well, I hope that teaches you a lesson, Deuce," Paul said, shaking his head sadly.

"And what lesson is that?" I asked. "Find out who has money riding each weekend?"

"No," Paul said, shaking his head again. "Every game matters. Even when they are five."

"They were four then," Tom said.

"So every game matters," Paul said. "And one other thing."

"What's that?" I asked.

"My kid is awful."

36

I stumbled home sometime around midnight and slept on the sofa because I didn't want to wake Julianne, getting home that late. It was the one night a month we slept apart, and it still felt like one night too many. I knew she wouldn't mind me coming in that late, but I never liked the idea of stirring her in the middle of the night if I didn't have to.

The next thing I knew, Carly was pouncing on my stomach.

"Daddy smells like beer!" she said, leaning her head down on my chest.

I cracked my eyes open. It felt like I'd just closed them, but the sun was up, so I knew I was wrong. And I probably did smell like beer.

Julianne joined us on the sofa, clutching her coffee mug. She slipped under my feet.

"Win or lose?" she asked.

"Even. Why are you still home?"

"Took the day off." She sipped from the mug. "And if you aren't losing too much money, then I guess we won't send you back to work full-time just yet." She winked at me.

"Daddy can't go to work!" Carly cried. "He takes care of me! I would be lonely!"

"I'm only teasing, kiddo," Julianne said.

Carly set her chin on my chest, our noses a few inches apart. "Don't go to work, okay, Daddy?"

"Okay. If you say so."

She rolled off and danced around the living room. "Yes! Daddy will stay home with me forever!"

Julianne and I laughed. I wanted to bottle those moments, not just for me, but so when Carly was a teenager and telling me to get out of her face—because, whether or not I liked it, that was going to happen—I could play back that video and show her that at one time, I was her favorite person on the planet.

"What about me?" Julianne asked. "Should I stay home?"

Carly froze in place in the middle of the room. "You go to work, though. So we can have food and stuff. Right?"

"Well, yeah," Julianne said, glancing at me. "But maybe I could do that and be at home a little more, too."

I saw something unfamiliar in Julianne's glance, something I wasn't sure I'd ever seen.

"You serious?" I asked.

"Could you do that?" Carly asked, wide-eyed. "Would we still be able to have chicken nuggets?"

Julianne smiled at her. "We will always have chicken nuggets for you, Carly. I promise."

Carly put a hand over her heart. "Okay, good. Because I love nuggets!"

She started dancing again.

Julianne looked at me. "Yes, I'm serious."

"About quitting your job?"

"Quitting the job I have," she said. "Yes. I've been thinking about it."

I leaned back into the sofa and took her words in. Ever since I'd known Julianne—really known her, not when we were kids and I was too stupid to notice her, but known her since I ran into her on a street in College Station—she'd placed an emphasis on her career. She didn't want to be a stay-at-home mom. She had too much energy, and she didn't have a need to stay home and do aerobics and gossip about people and things in town. She was certain that she could be a great mom, as well as a great lawyer.

And she was. She didn't come home and bury herself in an office full of work. She came home at night and she was a mom. She had far more energy than I'd ever had, and she didn't cheat Carly out of any of it. She was super lawyer and supermom, not to mention superwife.

When we'd learned she was pregnant with Carly, it had been an easy decision for me to leave my teaching job and for her to continue working. It was actually her idea because she was opposed to day care when we could obviously afford to have one of us stay at home. Her salary was the one we lived on, and I was more wired to stay at home. We made the decision in about nine seconds.

So hearing that she had any notion of staying home was huge breaking news to me.

"What does that mean?" I asked. "Quitting the job you have."

She snuggled onto the sofa next to me and

wrapped her arms around one of mine. "Don't worry. I'm not thinking about sending you back to the classroom."

"I'd go back," I said.

"No!" Carly yelled. "You just promised you'd stay home forever!"

"But I've always gotten to stay at home with you," I said. "Mommy hasn't gotten to do that, and maybe it's her turn." I looked at Julianne. "Might mean fewer nuggets, but I'd go back if that's what you want."

And I meant that. As much as I loved being at home, there was a fair amount of guilt that came with seeing Julianne leave every morning and miss out on the days with us. I appreciated that she was sacrificing her time with Carly to give it to me, but there was a part of me that wanted to give it back to her, to let her share in all the things I'd gotten to do with our daughter.

Julianne squeezed my arm tighter. "Thank you for saying that, but no. You are the greatest dad ever, and you belong at home with her."

"Then what are you talking about?"

"I've been thinking that maybe I need my own practice," she said. "Here. In town."

"In Rose Petal?"

She nodded. "Yep."

"But you're a partner. You just wanna leave that?"

"It's not the leaving," she said. "It's the things I'd be going to."

"Like?"

She pulled away from me and raised an eyebrow. "Do you not want me around more?"

I made a face. "You know I do. But this is all very un-Julianne like."

She smiled, then nodded. "Yeah, it is." She shrugged. "I don't know, Deuce. I really want another baby, and I don't want to work so hard and be gone so much for this one." She gestured at Carly, who was now lying on her back on the floor. "I feel like she got to this age in about five minutes, and I don't want to miss the next five minutes. That make sense?"

I pulled her back to me. "Yeah, it does. So do it."

"Easier said than done."

"No, it's not. If that's what you want, let's make it happen."

"Probably mean less money," she said. "Might be a little tight getting started."

"If it means having you around more, I can take it."

Carly jumped up and came over to us. She slapped one hand on my knee and another on Julianne's. She moved her eyes back and forth between us, and they were full of seriousness and gravity.

"We cannot tighten up on nuggets," she said.

37

The girls went into the kitchen to make pancakes, while I went upstairs to shower and wake up.

I dressed and sat down on the bed with my laptop, waiting for them to call me down. I powered up the computer and punched in the Web address Amber and Suzie had given me.

It didn't look much different than the tip sheet except that it had an account button. I followed the steps, and in five minutes I'd dropped two hundred bucks into my account and bet a hundred of it on two college football games for that morning. I wanted to get the ball rolling fast, and I figured the sooner I showed them that I was interested in betting, the sooner I might be able to gain their trust and get closer to getting access to Moises.

We ate a quick breakfast, and the girls headed out to do a little grocery shopping and a few other errands. Julianne never specifically asked me to stay home, but I was happy to let them have some Mommy-and-daughter time any time that I could.

I walked outside, thinking it might be a good day

to actually do some yard work, and was surprised to see Elliott sitting at the curb in his orange Bug.

He was wearing the horrible mustache and wig again.

I waved at him, and he got out of the car and came up the drive.

"The church money," he said without saying hello. "Moises doesn't have it."

"You know that for sure?"

"He says he doesn't." He looked around nervously. "Can we go inside?"

"Think someone is going to recognize you?"

"Those girls freak me out."

"Let's go in the backyard."

We walked around the side of the house, through the gate, and into the yard. We sat down in a couple of lawn chairs near the deck.

"He says he doesn't have it," Elliott said.

"Not what I was told," I said.

"Well, he wouldn't lie to me."

"No? Hate to tell you this, but he sorta seems like exactly the kind of guy who would lie to you."

Elliott shook his head violently. "No. Not over this."

"Why? How are you so sure?"

"I know my cousin."

A couple of bees buzzed our way, and I waved them away. I didn't think Elliott knew his cousin at all, really. I thought he had blinders on and refused to see what was going on with Moises.

"When did he start gambling?" I asked.

Elliott thought for a moment, his mouth twisting. "I don't know."

"What does he gamble on?" I asked.

"Sports. And other stuff."

"Which sports?"

"I don't really know."

"How long has he worked at the church?" I asked.

"Awhile."

"What's awhile?"

Elliott shifted in the chair. "I'm not sure."

"But you know your cousin."

His face flushed, and he looked away, staring at the grass for a while.

I wasn't trying to embarrass him, but I was trying to make a point. He seemed to be loyal to a fault, and I couldn't help but wonder if Moises was taking advantage of that. Family had a way of turning people blind in a hurry.

"Okay, I don't know everything about my cousin," Elliott finally said. "You are correct. But I don't believe he is lying about this."

"Why not?"

"One thing he showed me was his account," Elliott said. "For the bets. I know what he owed. If he stole all that money, he could've paid the girls off."

"Maybe he wanted extra."

"Moises isn't a bad person, Mr. Winters," Elliott said, his brows furrowing together. "This may seem bad, but he's not a bad person."

"I believe you, but a lot of this doesn't make sense."

"I understand that."

"And I'm just trying to figure it out. Not much about your cousin is making sense to me, and you are the only one taking his side."

"You are on his side, no?" Elliott asked.

I was starting to answer when I heard my name

shouted from the house. "Deuce? Where are you? Dammit, I need your help!"

"Out here, Dad," I yelled. I looked at Elliott, who was halfway out of the chair, his eyes wide with panic. "Relax. It's okay. It's my father."

My dad stormed out onto the deck, my mother's netbook in his hand. He started to say something, then fixed his eyes on Elliott.

"Son, that is the worst Halloween costume I've ever seen, and it ain't even October," he said.

"Dad."

"I mean, I could draw a mustache on you better than that if you need one."

"Dad, shut up."

Elliott's face took on a look of bewilderment. He didn't know what to make of my father.

Join the club.

My dad snapped his gaze to me and held out the netbook. "That damn Facebook again."

"What about it?"

"People keep asking your mother to be their friend," he barked.

"So?"

"She doesn't have that many friends," he said. "What do they really want?"

Elliott stood. "I should go."

"You don't have to."

"Do you know anything about Facebook?" my father asked him. "Doubt you would, given that god-awful costume, but there seem to be a lot of morons on this Facebook and you—"

"Dad, shut *up*," I said, cutting him off.

He frowned back and waited.

Elliott was already walking to the gate. "I will prove to you that my cousin is not lying."

"You don't have to do that."

"I feel like I do," Elliott said, pushing the gate open. "Then maybe you will help him."

"I'm already helping him," I said.

Elliott disappeared through the gate without saying anything else.

"Who the hell was that?" my father asked when the gate clanged shut.

"Just a guy I'm trying to help," I said.

"Well, you could start by telling him not to dress like a fool."

38

I convinced my father that Facebook friends weren't after my mom or his money or his investments or his granddaughter.

It took only an hour.

He left, and I called Victor to give him an update on what I'd done since I'd seen him last.

"Ten bucks says you'll never see your wife's money again," he said after I told him about placing the bets.

"Why's that?"

"Sorority girls running a betting biz?" he said, skepticism dripping from his words. "Gimme a break. That has *sham* written all over it."

"I think it's legit," I told him. "May not be legal, but I think it's legit."

"You aren't exactly known for your brains."

"And you aren't known for being able to reach the drinking glasses."

"Ha. I'm just saying, if it goes bad, don't say I didn't tell you so."

"I'll take the risk. You do any digging on them? The girls, I mean."

He hesitated. "I told you I thought this whole thing was a waste of time."

"I know. But I also know you can't help yourself sometimes and probably went home yesterday and did a little poking around. No pun intended."

He coughed and grumbled a bit. "Maybe I did."

"And?"

"Guess who the largest consumer group of Viagra buyers is?"

"I literally don't have any clue as to how to answer that."

"Male college students."

"You're serious?"

"Yeah, unfortunately. They got money, they watch too much porn, and they can't get it up."

"So they buy Viagra?"

"Not the real stuff. Too embarrassed, I'd guess. So they buy the cheap, knockoff crap that you can apparently get on any street corner."

"You seem to know a lot about this."

"Because I spent an hour on the computer, you big jackass," he snarled. "My parts are working just fine. Ask the missus. She'd be happy to tell you."

I imagined what I might hear, then tried to unimagine that because I didn't need nightmares.

"So maybe the girls have another business," I said.

"Their customers are probably into both," Victor said. "Dumb frat boys making stupid bets and then spending their winnings on boner pills."

"Is that the medical term on your prescription? Boner pills?"

"I don't know what the hell ya call them, because I ain't never tried 'em!"

I doubted that it would ever get old riling Victor up. It always brightened my day.

"I think you're right," I said. "That makes sense. And thanks for digging."

"Well, I didn't have anything to do, anyway," he said. "Victor Junior is sleeping so good now, I got a lot of free time again and I don't feel like a zombie anymore."

"Yeah? Swaddling is still working?"

"Man, we wrap that little dude up like a sausage every night, and he goes out like a light," he said. "Yeah, it's still working."

"Good. I'm glad."

"Yeah. Me, too. Thanks, I guess."

"Anytime. Happy to help. Oh, and I've got one other thing, too, that might help."

"Yeah? What's that?"

"Don't let him get into your boner pills."

He was cursing as he hung up.

39

I doubled my money.

Julianne called and said they were going to have lunch out and take their time getting home. I made myself at home on the sofa and turned on the football games, and in two hours' time, I won both bets I'd placed that morning.

I grabbed the laptop and logged into my account. The winnings were already there.

This wasn't a sham. These girls were flat-out legitimate bookies, and they made good within fifteen minutes of the end of the last game. They knew what they were doing, and they had enough cash to cover the bets they were taking.

And I thought that also made them dangerous.

Maybe there was a little more urgency in finding Moises.

I went to my desk and grabbed the stack of e-mails that Victor originally gave me from Moises's computer, and sifted through them again. The first time I looked through them, I wasn't sure what I was looking for. This time, I still wasn't sure, but I felt like I at least had a little more information about Moises to go on.

The fifth one in was the first to catch my attention.

It was from Joel Metairie. Joel was an acquaintance in town, someone I knew just from living in Rose Petal. I knew he had kids at the elementary school, but I wasn't sure what ages they were. And he apparently hosted the poker game that Moises was kicked out of.

The e-mail was from several months back.

Seven o'clock start time, boys, it read. You bring the beer and your money, and I'll have the pizzas and your money by the end of the night. Two-bill buy-in will get you started. Let me know if you're in or out. Joel.

I grabbed my computer again and punched Joel's name into a search engine, looking for a phone number. I didn't get a number, but it did bring up an address just a few minutes away.

I changed into my running clothes, tied on my shoes, and headed out.

The summer sun hadn't completely permeated the air yet, so I was able to breathe as I ran through the neighborhood, sweating out the alcohol and wings from the previous night. I waved to several neighbors as I went, raising my hand up as I huffed and puffed along. I didn't know all their names, but they were people I saw on a daily basis, the kind of people who always smiled and waved back and gave me the feeling that they'd let me borrow a piece of lawn equipment or kitchen utensil if I needed it. I complained a lot about the idiosyncrasies of Rose Petal, but it was nice living in a place where nearly everyone was happy to loan you their weed whacker.

I slowed down as I approached the address I'd found for Joel Metairie. I recognized him in his driveway, washing a massive Ford F-350 pickup. His Cowboys T-shirt and cargo shorts were soaked in water, and his thinning hair was sticking out in multiple places. He was big, with broad shoulders and a forming beer belly, and looked exactly like the kind of guy who would drive a truck the size of an elephant.

I walked up to the edge of the driveway, catching my breath, and he turned my way as he picked up the bucket full of soapy water. He started to give me a cursory wave, then realized he knew me.

"Hey, Deuce," he said, lifting his chin up. "How's it going?"

"Hey, Joel," I said, holding my hand up. "Good." I pointed at the truck. "They kick you outta the car wash?"

He grinned and set down the bucket. "They see me coming, and they put out the CLOSED signs. Afraid I'll use all the water."

He came down to the edge of the drive, and we shook hands. We talked about school and kids for a moment, before I attempted to make the awkward transition. It was an investigation skill I had yet to master.

"I've got a weird question for you, if you don't mind," I said.

Confusion rooted on his face. "Weird? Like what?"

"I heard you have a regular poker game."

Confusion changed to a smile. "Oh, heck yeah. You want in? Once a month, decent money, a lot of laughs. Some good players, too."

I shook my head. "Nah, I'm not good enough for that, to tell you the truth."

"All the more reason you should come," he said, winking.

"If you can't spot the sucker, you are the sucker," I said. "That'd be me."

"Ah, it's all in fun. You should come."

"I wanted to ask you about one of the guys in your group."

He shrugged, the confusion back. "Okay."

"Moises Huber?"

The confusion dissipated to a look of annoyance. "Oh. Yeah."

"He plays in your game?"

Joel shifted his weight from one foot to the other and pulled at his wet shirt. "Played. Not anymore."

"You mind me asking why?"

"Are you a friend of his?"

"No, not really," I said.

"Because he is not welcome here, and I don't mean to be rude, Deuce, but anybody who is friends with that guy just isn't welcome at my home."

"Understood. I only know him from soccer."

He nodded. "Yeah. That was how I knew him originally. One of the other guys that plays with us told him about the game. He wanted in right away."

I didn't say anything.

"So he came a couple of times," Joel explained. "Seemed like a decent enough guy. Maybe third or fourth time, he showed up short."

"Short?"

He started to say something, then stopped. "You do, like, private eye work or something like that, right?"

I nodded.

"I don't wanna get in trouble for running a game," he said. "It really is just for fun."

"Don't worry," I said. "I'm not asking so I can bust up your game. I play in a much smaller game on a regular basis, so I get it. I'm really just interested in Huber."

"Did he really take all of the soccer money?"

"I'm really not sure. I'm trying to find out."

Joel nodded. "Fair enough. Okay, so he came up short. He didn't have enough to cover his bets for that night."

"Gotcha."

"And, you know, one time, no big deal," he continued. "It happens. You get caught up, and things get a little crazy, and boom. You owe more than you brought." He shrugged. "No big deal. You make arrangements with whoever you owe, and you pay 'em during the week or next time we get together. I've done it. Most of the guys have done it. Not like we send out some guy to collect or anything like that. Everyone's friends, and no one wants to be the guy that stiffs someone else, you know? And a couple of the guys, they don't like to play for the big money. So they stay out of those pots. Which is cool, too. There's no pressure. Guys bet what they want, and we drink a bunch of beer and have a bunch of laughs."

"Sounds a lot like my game," I said.

"It probably is, Deuce," Joel said. "Probably just the amount of money in play that's different."

"Sounds like it."

Joel nodded, pleased that we were on the same page. "So, anyway, he comes up short. He gets real apologetic and says he'll run to the ATM, blah, blah, blah. We tell him to relax. It's no big deal. He can pay Chuck later in the week or whatever they work out. It was Chuck Blasingame that he owed that night. You know Chuck?"

"Know the name."

"Good guy. Has a roofing business. Good guy. Anyway, he tells Chuck he'll get to him later in the week." Joel's expression clouded. "But he didn't."

"Okay."

"Chuck sends him an e-mail or two, giving him a hard time, mainly just kidding him, because Chuck honestly doesn't care," Joel said. "Each time, Huber says he forgot, or some crap like that. He'll get it right to him. Never does."

Joel pulled at his wet shirt again. "So next month rolls around, and Huber shows up. But he brings Chuck's money, so we're all good. Chuck's almost embarrassed to take his money at that point. You know what I mean?"

"Sure."

"Then he comes up short again that night. Goes all in on a big pot and can't cover when he busts out."

"What's big?"

He thought for a moment. "Think it was around a grand."

"Whoa."

"Like I said, we don't limit. Guys put in play what they're comfortable playing. Or losing."

I nodded. The thought of a thousand dollars being in play at my game made my stomach turn. I liked gambling, but not when the stakes were the size of mortgages.

"This time it's not Chuck, though," Joel said. "It's Kane Delacorte. Know him?"

"Nope."

"Well, Kane's a bit of a red ass. Decent guy but kinda serious. And he's irritated that he's getting stiffed. Some of it was that it happened the month before, but mostly because Kane wants his money." Joel chuckled. "And he immediately says he wants it by the end of the week."

"What did Huber say?"

"Said no problem, he would have it to him, and would bring it to his house by midweek," Joel said. "But, of course, he didn't."

Two kids on bikes pedaled by and hollered at Joel. He waved back.

"So Kane starts getting on him pretty good," he explained. "E-mails him like twice a day. Tries to call him. Huber keeps putting him off. Tells him he's busy. That kind of crap. But he never comes through."

"Did he show up the next month?"

Joel nodded. "Yep. With Kane's money. But Kane's pissed, okay? Doesn't wanna let him play. Huber offers to pay his buy-in for that night, because he feels bad. A little weird considering it took him so long to pay up, but he's got the extra two hundred to cover Kane. So we let him."

I had to wonder if Moises was placing other bets to cover his losses. I knew that was a common habit of gamblers who got in too deep. They were always just one big payday away from being flush.

"So we get to the end of the night, and Huber's actually done pretty well," Joel said. "He's up pretty good. And we get to one last big pot. It's, like, two in the morning, and there's about three grand on the table."

"Three grand?" I said.

Joel held his hands up in a what-can-you-do way. "Hey. These guys like poker, and they are big boys."

I imagined Julianne coming after me with a hatchet if I gambled that kind of money in my dumb little game.

"So there's three grand in, and Huber goes all in," Joel said. "Room gets kinda quiet. Kane finally says, 'Hey, man, do not go all in if you can't cover tonight, because that ain't cool.'"

I nodded.

"Huber says it's no problem, he's flush, and if he loses, he can pay up on the spot," Joel said, his expression hardening. "No waiting or late payoffs. So we said okay."

I waited.

"And it got down to him and Chuck," Joel said. "And you could just tell Huber thought he had it won. He's a decent player, but not much of a poker face. He laid down four queens and started reaching for the chips. But Chuck started giggling and dropped four kings. Entire room exploded."

I knew that feeling. Anytime someone got surprised in our game, there was much celebrating and razzing. They were the highlights of every night.

"Huber just went pale," Joel said, frowning. "And I just knew he'd lied. I knew he didn't have it to cover, and I probably should've asked him to show the money before he played the hand, but I didn't. He gets all flustered, makes a show of checking his wallet and acting like he's confused because there isn't as much money in there as he thought there was."

I shook my head.

"Chuck being Chuck," Joel continued, "he tells him not to worry about it. Absolutely lets him off the hook. But Kane and a couple of the other guys were pissed. And I'll be honest. So was I." His eyes narrowed. "He flat-out lied to us, and that was the part I didn't like."

"What did you guys do?"

"Kane was ready to kick his ass," Joel said. "But I walked him outside and told him that he owed that money to Chuck, and after he paid it, he was not welcome back. I didn't threaten him, but I wasn't nice about it, either. The guy was ruining what's supposed to be a fun night."

"Wow," I said, just shaking my head. "He ever pay Chuck?"

Joel shook his head. "Nope. Not a penny. Just disappeared."

40

I went home and found a voice mail on my cell.

"Hey, big winner," Amber's voice said. "You did well today! Awesome! Let me know if you wanna play with some of that other money we talked about. Later!"

I wondered if she called all her winners like that or if she called just the ones who had promised more money.

I wondered that rhetorically, of course.

After I showered and changed clothes, I grabbed a notepad and stretched out on the sofa, waiting for the girls to return.

One trick Victor had showed me was to write down everything I knew about the case I was in the middle of, even if I had the details clear in my head. He maintained that putting them down on paper let you see them a little differently and sometimes led to finding things you couldn't see in your head. I begrudgingly had to admit that it had worked on more than one occasion and I'd started doing it dutifully each time we worked a new case.

Of course, I didn't tell him that.

It took me thirty minutes to get down everything I knew, which didn't feel like much. The two things that stuck out to me were the mismatched amounts of money—the money the Huber cousins said was stolen versus the money they were accused of stealing—and the missing Viagra-filled trophies. Regardless of whether or not the money amounts were correct, if we could locate the trophies, I felt like we would at least have some leverage to get Moises back and see what he'd done with the money. I wasn't exactly sure what that would mean for the soccer association and Elliott's job, but I wasn't sure that was my responsibility, either.

The girls came home and we did dinner and I gave Carly a bath and she was falling asleep in the tub, she was so tired. I crawled into bed with her, but she was out before we even cracked a book. I lay with her in the dark until I heard her snoring, then snuck quietly out of the room.

Julianne was stretched out on the bed in our room, in an A&M T-shirt and sweats with her laptop across her legs.

I slid onto the bed next to her and kissed her neck. "Is tonight a green night?" I whispered.

She smiled. "I have no idea. But it doesn't need to be."

I pulled back. "Wait, I thought we were trying to have a baby."

"We are," she said. "But I feel like just strictly going by the charts and graphs is creating too much . . . pressure." She looked away from the screen at me. "For me. Not you."

"I don't mind them."

"I know you don't," she said, kissing my forehead. "But we don't need them. At least not all the time."

"If you say so." I kissed her neck again. "As long as you aren't rejecting me."

"Never," she said. "Give me one minute."

I looked at the computer screen. It was some sort of contract. "What's that?"

"My partner agreement."

I blinked. "You're looking at your options?"

She nodded. "I'm going to talk to James this week."

"You mean quit?"

"I'm gonna let him know it's on the horizon."

"You're not even pregnant yet."

She closed the laptop, set it on the nightstand, and curled up next to me. "I had fun with Carly today. Just me and her, running around, wasting time, just having fun. I don't mean without you. I just mean . . ."

"I know what you mean. Really. It's good."

She nodded. "It was good. And I just decided that whether or not we have another baby, I don't want to be working my ass off for the next ten years while she grows up. Baby or no baby, I'm done with the grind."

I put my arms around her. "Good."

"Yeah?"

"Absolutely."

"I won't drive you nuts if I'm around more?"

"You might, but I'll adjust."

She smiled and moved tighter against me. "Good.

I don't know why, Deuce, but I'm just feeling the mommy pull."

"Nothing wrong with that."

"It's just weird. For me."

It probably was, and it was probably even weirder for her to say it out loud, to admit it. But I was glad she wasn't pretending it wasn't there. I was glad that she was being honest with herself and with me. I wanted her to do whatever made her happy.

"There's nothing weird about you," I said. "I would know."

Her hands found the small of my back, and she pulled me close. Her lips attached to my neck, and goose bumps formed on my skin.

"You know how much I like to be flattered," she whispered to me.

"Yes. I do."

"I think you're gonna get lucky."

"I was hoping."

"Daddy?"

We both froze at the sound of Carly's voice.

Julianne sat up. "What's going on, kiddo?"

"I had a bad dream."

I pushed myself up. She was standing in the doorway, sleepy eyed and disheveled, holding her stuffed white cat by the tail.

"You want me to take you back to bed?" I offered.

She shook her head. "No. Can I get in your bed?"

I looked at Julianne, and she smiled at me, raising her eyebrows.

I sighed. "Yep. Come on, babe."

Carly hopped up on the bed and crawled in between us. She burrowed under the covers and nestled between our bodies, hugging her kitty. Julianne looked at me over the top of our daughter's head, and I looked at her, longingly.

"Tomorrow," she whispered.

I sighed again and nodded as I lay my head down on the pillow. "Tomorrow."

41

Belinda was parked in front of my house when I
returned from dropping Carly at VBS Monday. She
pushed herself out of her truck as soon as she saw me
walking up the block, and was standing in the drive
by the time I got there, each of her massive legs
planted on the concrete like tree roots.

"Where do we stand, Deuce?" she asked, already
sweating in the early morning sunlight.

"We're in my driveway, Belinda."

She frowned, finding no humor in my humor.
"You know what I mean."

I gave her the short, cleaned-up version, leaving
out the specific details about where we thought
Moises was and what the trophies were housing.

Her lips formed a flat line across her mouth.
"Okay. That isn't much."

"No, it's really not. But that's what we've got."

She chewed on her bottom lip for a moment. "We
don't have money to pay the officials this weekend,
Deuce. Or pay for field usage, because that's due
on Friday, before the games."

"So what happens?"

"I'm thinking we gotta cancel."

My stomach turned. I knew how disappointed Carly would be if there was no game on Saturday. She'd be confused, upset, but ultimately, we'd be able to pacify her and she'd be all right. Not all kids would react the same way. Some would be crushed.

And that was in the short term. The long-term damage would have a greater effect. Even if the money was recovered and the league was reestablished as financially viable, the league's reputation would be stained forever. They would forever be known as the soccer league that had to shut down because they had no money, and fair or not, the league would carry that around its neck forever.

"What's the time frame?" I asked.

Her mouth twisted like she'd just bitten into a rotten lemon. "I think I have to start composing the e-mail today. Logistically, we have to let our coaches and families know right away. We can't wait until the last minute to drop that kind of mass cancellation on them."

"We do with weather."

"It's different, and you know it," she said. "If the weather is crappy, they know to call the weather line and check the Web site. Weather is gonna be fine this weekend." Her features softened. "And, honestly, we owe them the truth. It's their money we've lost. They should know."

Belinda was right. They had a right to know, as uncomfortable as it might be. Being that it was fee driven, it was essentially their league. If it was falling into insolvency, they deserved the right to get upset about it.

I wiped the sweat off my forehead. "When's the absolute last minute you feel comfortable sending out the e-mail to everyone?"

She thought for a moment. "Some people won't get the e-mail, so we'll still need to make some phone calls. I'd say Wednesday night is my drop-dead date."

That gave me forty-eight hours. Not ideal, but maybe it was just time to push the envelope and see what happened.

"Okay," I said. "Wait until then. I'll see what I can do. And then I'll touch base with you on Wednesday afternoon. If I don't have anything for you, you can send out the notice. Sound all right?"

Belinda sighed, and her massive body sagged. "No. Not really. But if that's all we got, that's all we got."

"Even if I find Moe, you know there's no guarantee the money's still around, right?"

She trudged slowly toward her truck. "I know. But at least if you find him, I'll be able to beat his ass."

42

I showered, ate some toast, finished the pot of coffee, and grabbed my cell phone.

I punched in the number I wanted, left a voice mail, and waited.

It rang three minutes later.

"Hey!" Amber screeched through the phone. "How *are* you? You had *such* a great day on Saturday! So happy for you!"

It was like having my own personal cheerleader.

"Yeah, I did," I said. "Thanks."

"You must have done this before!"

"Can't say that I have."

"Well, I certainly hope it's not beginner's luck!"

Amber was either a great actress or really didn't mind losing money.

"Me, either, but I'm ready to find out," I said.

"Yay!"

"I mentioned the other day that I might be interested in placing some bigger bets," I said. "You told me that maybe I should wait. Are we at that point yet?"

"I think we might be able to work that out now that you are a totally valued customer."

"Here's the deal," I said. "I'm not really comfortable putting this kind of money into an account. Because I worry about people finding it. Know what I mean?"

"Not really," she answered, sounding genuinely confused.

"It's a fairly large amount of money. I don't want any record that the IRS might be able to track. Receipts, deposits, those kinds of things."

"Gotcha," Amber said, catching up. "So what are we talking here?"

"I'd prefer to just bring you the cash I'd like to put in play."

She was silent for a moment. "Hmmm. Hang on a second, all right?"

"All right."

The line went quiet, and I was pretty sure she'd put me on mute. I wondered if Suzie was standing nearby, scowling and being surly.

"Okay," she said, her voice bursting back through the line. "How much are we talking about?"

"Uh, six figures," I said, saying the first thing that came to mind.

"Hold on."

The line went quiet again. I needed to decide exactly what amount I'd give her if she came back and wanted the specifics. I wanted to make it sound realistic but still sizable. The problem was, I didn't have any idea what kind of bets they saw on a regular basis.

It ended up not mattering.

"All right," Amber's voice shouted through the

phone. "Since you've been so totally awesome so far, we feel totally comfortable doing this with you. Because we wanna help you out, ya know?"

"Of course."

"Know which games you're interested in yet?"

"No. I haven't checked the lines yet. But I will today, and I'll let you know. Then maybe we can set something up?"

"Totes!" Amber squealed. "Call me! Later!"

43

I hung up, and my phone chirped immediately.

"I got info, Stilts," Victor barked at me.

"On what?"

"Alpha Gamma Tau."

"Excuse you?"

"Alpha Gamma Tau."

"I have no idea what you're talking about."

"Your sorority girl bookies, you big dope!" he
yelled. "The sorority is Alpha Gamma Tau."

"At SMU?"

"Yep."

"How do you know?"

He made a sound like he wanted to vomit. "Really?
After all this time, you're still questioning me?"

He had a point. "Sorry. Okay. Alpha Gamma Tau.
They're running the betting?"

"Yeah. Been doing it for a while, apparently. It's
out there. People know."

"So it's overt?"

"I wouldn't say overt, but it's not a tight secret.
Took me about two hours to run them down."

"That long?"

"Ha."

"You wanna go with me to meet them?" I asked.

"Why are you going to meet them?"

I explained my idea and my urgency.

"I think that's a terrible plan," he said.

"Why?"

"Because it's not even a plan."

"I think if I put them on the spot, I can get them to give up Huber."

"But maybe not the money, and isn't that what you really need?"

Smart midgets were the worst.

"I'll worry about that part when I get to it," I said.

"Again. Horrible plan."

"Do you want to go or not?"

"I probably should, in case the sorority girls are too tough for you," he said, and I could tell he was grinning. "And they probably need someone handsome to look at after looking at your horrific mug."

"Who are you gonna bring?"

"I don't need anybody but me, baby," he said. "One look at this face and they'll be in love."

"Or cardiac arrest."

"When are we going?"

"Today."

"Today?"

"Did I stutter?"

"When?"

"Sooner rather than later."

"So I should head your way now?"

"As much as I hate to say yes . . . yes."

"Fine. But I'm driving."

"We can argue about that when you get here."

"I'm not riding in your stinking van, because I always end up on the floor in that thing," he barked.

"We'll figure it out when you get here."

"There ain't nothing to figure out, Stilts. You can get in my car or not."

"Whatever. Just get here."

"Keep your giant pants on. I'll be there soon."

"Great. I won't look forward to it."

He cackled before he hung up.

44

I arranged with my mom to pick up Carly at camp in case I was gone for the better part of the afternoon. I didn't want to get stuck in the middle of anything and then not be able to get to her. My mom was more than happy to meet her at VBS, and I knew Carly would love the surprise of having her grandmother pick her up.

I was going to call Amber back but then realized that made no sense. I didn't want her to have any warning, and I didn't want her to know I knew where she was. I didn't need to scare them off. I hated to admit it, but there were times where I felt completely at a loss as to what I was doing as an investigator, and I had to rely on Victor to save my rear end.

An engine roared into my driveway, and a horn blasted longer than necessary.

Victor.

I walked outside. The top was down on his convertible, and heavy metal blared from the speakers. He saw me and turned it up.

"Let me drive," I yelled over the music, coming up to the side of the car.

He cupped his hand around his ear like he couldn't hear me.

"Let me drive!"

He frowned at me. "I'm leaving in five seconds, with or without you."

Against my better judgment, I opened the door and slid into the passenger seat of his Miata. Blocks were attached to the pedals, and he pressed on the accelerator, revving the engine, grinning like a shark.

"Just drive," I said.

He cackled and threw it into reverse, roaring out of the driveway.

He hit the button on his door panel, and the windows pushed up, buffeting the wind noise.

"You know where you're going?" I asked.

He turned down the stereo and nodded. "Greek Row. It's right near the campus. All the little rich kids living in mini-mansions, drinking and doin' who knows what."

In all the years I had lived in the Dallas area, I had never been to SMU's Greek Row. I had heard about it but had never had a reason to go. Going to college down at A&M, it would've been heresy to have visited the campus when I was home. And once I'd graduated, there was no reason to go check out the antics on their row.

We hit the highway, and Victor maneuvered us into the fast lane. "You still stuck on your plan that's not a plan?"

"Yeah. I don't have anything better. And they're gonna have to cancel soccer if we don't find some way to get the money back."

He made a face. "It's just soccer."

I laughed. "Just you wait until your son is old enough to play. Your entire life is going to revolve around whatever activities he's in. And they will seem more important than anything else going on in your life."

"Not a chance."

I shook my head and chuckled. Everyone thought that. But then it happened over night. No more movies, no more dates, no more happy hours. Everything was about game times and snack schedules and birthday parties and playdates. Your needs and wants became completely subordinate to those of your child.

"Whatever," I said. "I don't want them to cancel soccer, and if I can help prevent that, I'm going to. And we are up against it in terms of time. So I think being direct is the best route."

He shrugged his little shoulders. "If you say so. But I'm telling you, if these girls have any heat behind them, it could get sticky."

"What do you mean by heat?"

He switched lanes quickly, and we swerved around an old Honda. "I'm just still not buying that these girls are really running this. I think they might be fronting for someone else."

"Like who?"

"Like who knows? Someone who places the bets and knows what they're doing and is making a nice tidy profit without showing their face." He shrugged again. "Plenty of those in the world. And using the girls is actually pretty smart."

I thought that, too. The girls—or at least Amber—were outgoing and flirtatious. Guys would go to them and not want to look like fools. They'd overbet, play more than they should, just because they'd think it might impress. And I couldn't think of anyone less likely to be suspected of running a gambling ring than a bunch of wealthy sorority girls.

Victor gunned the engine again, and the Miata shot across two lanes.

"I'd prefer not to die today," I said.

"Lucky you're with me, then."

"Right."

"What's the plan if they deny anything?" he asked, glancing over at me. "If they evade? Because it's entirely possible that that dude with the bad wig and mustache could be lying to you."

"He wasn't lying about the gambling part, with the girls."

"Most people who lie tell a little bit of the truth. It buys them time."

I didn't say anything.

"The people who lie all the time?" Victor said. He waved a hand dismissively. "They're easy to spot, because everything sounds like a lie. But the ones who mix in the lies with the truth? Those are the ones who are good at lying."

I hated how Victor could so easily make me doubt myself.

"I don't know, then," I said. "I don't have a backup plan."

"Of course you don't." He shook his head. "Telling you. This whole thing makes me nervous."

"Just get us there in one piece," I said. "I'll figure it out."

"Oh, that makes me feel great," he said, frowning.

"People who just plan to figure it out are usually the ones who end up dead in the movies."

"This isn't a movie."

"Feels like one. A really bad one."

"Just drive."

Twenty minutes later he was parallel parking the Miata at a curb beneath towering oaks. The street was lined with mansions and pillars and Greek letters, and I was pretty sure if the wind blew in the right direction, the smell of money would drift along the tree limbs. Expensive cars lined the street like there was a foreign auto show in town, and college students lounged on the steps of their houses, their eyes hidden behind mirrored sunglasses and their hands occupied by plastic red cups.

"You go to college?" I asked Victor as we got out.

"What? You think they don't let my kind go to college?"

"I was just asking."

He hitched up his pants, pants that would've been nice walking shorts on me. "Nah, I didn't go. I had better things to do."

"Like?"

"Like getting a job and getting on with my life," he said, scowling at me. "Stop being so nosy."

For as much time as I spent with Victor, I knew very little about him. I made a mental note to revisit the college conversation when time allowed in the future.

We walked two blocks before we came upon the Alpha Gamma Tau house. Four giant white pillars buttressed wide brick steps. A nicely manicured lawn spread out along the front, and several girls were sitting on towels on the grass, all sporting a shirt or tank top with their Greek letters across their chest.

They eyed us with what appeared to be a mixture of curiosity and annoyance, whispering behind their hands and pointing at Victor.

"Hi, ladies," I said. "Is Amber around?"

A blonde with long hair and tan legs snorted. "Which one?"

"Uh, the one that hangs out with Suzie."

They all chuckled, and I felt like the dumb kid in class.

"You're really gonna have to be more specific," the blonde said.

The others nodded, affirming my need for specificity.

I gave them physical descriptions, and a girl with short black hair nodded. "Oh, sure. I don't know if they're here or not." She moved her eyes from me to Victor. "And who are you, cutie?"

Victor puffed out his chest. "Victor Anthony Doolittle." He removed his hat and bowed. "At your service, ladies."

They all giggled and immediately reached for their phones. They all held them up, and shutters snapped across the lawn.

Victor stood and replaced the hat on his head. "Now, how might we find Amber and Suzie?"

"You don't like us?" the dark-haired one asked. "What's wrong with us?"

"Au contraire," Victor said. "Nothing's wrong with you. I'd be happy to come back and sit with you and regale you with tales of my daring after we find Amber and Suzie."

His new lady friend pouted. "You're making me feel like second choice."

Her friends joined in the pout.

Victor puffed out his chest again. "Ladies, I promise, you are not second choice, but we've promised your friends that we'd come visit them first. After that . . ." He turned his palms up. "Who knows where the day will take us?"

They squealed with delight, and I couldn't tell if they were mocking him or genuinely excited.

I felt slightly nauseous.

The blonde stood up. "I'll go see if I can find them. Wait here."

She hopped up the steps and disappeared into the mansion.

A girl with long red hair pushed her sunglasses down her nose. "I like your hat."

"Most everyone does," Victor said.

"Bull," I muttered.

"Can I wear it?" Red asked.

He removed it from his head and flipped it to her. She caught it and plopped it on her head.

Her friends applauded.

"I think it looks better on you," Victor said, grinning.

"Oh, no way," she said, shaking her head. "Not possible."

"Anything's possible."

Red tilted the hat upward. "You should come to our party tonight."

Victor raised an eyebrow. "Party?"

"Sure. It's in the backyard," she said. "Kegger. You can be my date."

"I saw him first, Megan," the dark-haired one spat.

"Whatever, Missy," Red, aka Megan, said.

"I'll be sure to tell Robby, then," Missy hissed.

Megan shrugged like it didn't matter.

"Ladies, ladies," Victor said, holding out his hands. "Please. Let's not fight over me."

"And he's married," I blurted out.

Both of the girls looked at me like I was an alien.

I felt the color rush into my face. "Well, he is."

"Even hotter," Megan whispered.

Missy nodded.

I tried not to throw up.

Before anyone could say anything else, the blonde emerged from the house. She perched on the top step.

"They aren't here," she said.

"Any idea when they're coming back?" I asked.

"No, but they said you could come to them," she said. "If you want."

I looked at Victor. He shrugged.

"Sure," I said.

She gave us an address. I looked at Victor.

"That isn't around here, is it?" he said.

She shook her head. "No. They're working on a service project. It's in South Dallas."

"Okay. We'll find it," Victor said. He turned to his audience on the grass. "Ladies, until we meet again."

They both sat up like cats about to pounce.

"Yeah," Megan whispered.

"Until we meet again," Missy whispered.

Creepy.

45

"That was just weird," I said.

"What? That they weren't there?"

"No. That they liked you."

We were flying down the 35, Victor weaving us in and out of cars that were doing normal speeds.

He smiled, and his teeth shone in the sunshine. "I'm a sexual magnet."

"Stop. That's just gross."

"No, it's true. My wife? She can't get enough of me."

"I've already had enough of you."

"Your jealousy is ugly."

"So is your face."

He cackled as he zipped across three lanes and took the exit he wanted.

The area we were in couldn't have been more different from the Park Cities area around SMU. Pillars and manicured lawns were replaced by low-slung ranch homes, misshapen garage doors, and networks of weeds. The cars on the streets were on their last legs, held together by duct tape and crossed fingers. We were maybe fifteen miles away, but we might as well have been in another universe.

"This must be some kind of service project," Victor muttered.

"Probably like a Habitat for Humanity thing," I said. "Where they build a house for someone who needs one."

"Couldn't they do it in a nicer looking place?"

"Don't worry. I'll protect you."

"I don't need you, Stilts. And I ain't afraid, either."

"If you say so."

Victor followed the directions on his GPS through a maze of neighborhood streets, each row of houses growing a little less cared for each time we turned. I was having a hard time envisioning Amber and Suzie being thrilled to come into this area of town to do good. I knew most Greek organizations required a certain number of service hours each year, but I had to wonder if they hadn't tried for something else and got stuck with something that didn't please them.

The Miata slowed, and Victor guided us to the curb.

He raised an eyebrow. "This is it."

A rectangular mass of brick and shingles was masquerading as a house. The glass in the two front windows was cracked, and the yard was a wide expanse of thick dirt and clumps of thistle. Two weathered and broken rocking chairs sat on the front stoop, which was barely big enough to hold both. The front door hung crooked on the hinges.

"Doesn't look like they've done much to service it," Victor noted wryly.

I could see movement behind the dusty, cracked windows. "Maybe they've just started."

"Well, they're gonna be here awhile, then."

We got out and walked up the concrete path that bisected the yard. Except it wasn't so much a path as a trail of busted hunks of concrete.

I pushed one of the broken rockers aside and knocked on the door.

Feet shuffled behind the door, and it swung open.

Amber held up a hand in greeting, another hand perched on her hip. "Hey!"

"Hi, Amber," I said. I motioned to Victor. "This is my friend Victor."

Her smile widened, and she put her hands on her knees. "Aren't you just the cutest thing ever?"

"I pretty much am, yeah," Victor said.

"Do you go by midget? Or little person?"

"I go by Victor," he said, his smile fading.

"Of course you do!" Amber squealed. "Hello, Victor!"

I couldn't tell whether he was happy to be the center of her attention or annoyed at her ignorance.

She stood up. "I didn't know you were coming. Or bringing a friend."

"Well, after we talked, I was feeling a bit impatient," I said. "The money was getting heavy in my pockets. If you know what I mean."

"Oh, do I," she said, grinning.

"And Victor was at my house," I continued. "I hire him to do landscaping. . . ."

"What the . . . ?" he said.

"Small bushes, not the tall trees, obviously. And he wondered where I was going, and I know he's a big sports fan, so I thought he might be able to, you know, participate, as well."

"I'm gonna kill you," he muttered.

"We could hire you to do the landscaping at the house!" Amber exclaimed. She clapped her hands together. "That would be so totally fun!"

"I keep him on a tight schedule, but I'm sure you could work something out," I said, enjoying myself.

"Def!"

"Can we come in?" I asked.

Her eyes shifted away from me. "Sure. We're all out back." She stepped aside to let us pass.

The interior of the house matched the exterior. Half of the carpeting was missing, and most of the furniture looked at least thirty years old. Holes in the plaster dotted the walls like a puzzle, and what little paint I saw was cracked and flaking. The room felt damp and cool, and a musty odor hung in the air.

Which I thought was a bit odd since they were supposedly cleaning it up.

"You guys just start working on this house?" I asked.

"Working on it?"

"For your service project?" I said. "That's what the girls at your house told us you were doing."

"Oh, right!" Amber said. "Service project. Totally. We've just started. So it's obviously still pretty icky."

"Icky's one word for it," Victor said.

I followed Victor through a torn-up kitchen missing all its appliances and to a back door with a dirty curtain covering the window. He reached up, opened it, and we stepped outside.

I surveyed the scene in front of me and felt stupid.

Victor turned to me and confirmed my stupidity. "You idiot."

46

Suzie used the gun she was holding to motion us toward two weather-beaten deck chairs. "Sit."

By my count, I saw six girls with guns. Most of them were wearing their sorority letters and supercute denim shorts. They were all holding small-caliber handguns, and they were pointed directly at us.

"I'll come up with a plan," Victor mimicked. "I'll figure it out." He sat down in the chair with a disgusted sigh.

"What's going on?" I asked, sitting down next to him.

"That's what we'd like to know," Suzie said, frowning.

Amber sat down in a chair across from us, crossed her legs, and smiled. "So what's up, guys?"

"Yeah," I said. "What's up?"

She tilted her head to the side. "Seriously."

"Amber, all your sorority sisters are pointing guns at me," I said.

"Us," Victor corrected. "Pointing guns at us."

"Right. Us," I said. "We came here to place some bets with you, and now I have no idea what's going on."

She looked at Victor. "And you're sticking with this story, too, cutie-pie?"

"It's all we got," Victor said.

"Oh my gawd, yeah, it is," she said, giggling. "And it's totally not much."

Her confidence and command were unnerving. I was beginning to realize that I had severely underestimated the girls of Alpha Gamma Tau, despite warning myself to not underestimate them.

Amber lifted her chin at one of the girls aiming at us. "Go get him."

The girl nodded, lowered the gun, and skipped around the corner of the house.

"Get who?" I asked.

Amber's phone dinged, and she pulled it out of her pocket. She smiled and looked at Victor. "Megan wants to know if you'll go to our fall formal with her."

"You're gonna ask me this with guns in my face?" he said.

"She's totally into you. Majorly."

He turned to me. "You suck. Majorly. I'm rethinking our partnership. Immediately."

"Partnership?" Amber asked, leaning forward. "Oh my gawd! Do you two, like, *like* each other?"

"Jesus Christ, no!" Victor said, inching away from me.

The girls with the guns giggled.

"Oh, good," Amber said. "Megan would be crushed. Anyway, let me know, 'kay?"

Victor rolled his eyes.

"Amber, what's going on?" I asked. "Why are we here?"

"Totally good question," she said, winking at me. "You should totally answer it."

She was calm, cool, and collected. There was no anxiety, no worry, no fear. She knew she had us, and she was comfortable being in that position.

I was not.

Before I could respond, I heard footsteps coming from where she'd sent her gun-wielding sorority sister. Part of me expected to see Moises Huber, now thinking this was where they'd kept him. I wasn't sure what the other half of me expected to see.

Half of me was right, and half of me was shocked.

In front of the armed sorority sister were both Moises Huber and his cousin, Elliott. I sorta knew how one got there, but I had no clue how the other had fallen into this predicament.

Moe looked a little tired, but other than that, he seemed fine. He held up a hand in greeting. "Hey, Deuce."

"Moe."

Elliott was staring at his feet.

"Guys, just have a seat right there, 'kay?" Amber said sweetly, waving her hand at the stairs that came up to the patio. "Lizzie, keep 'em covered. Just in case they wanna get silly or something."

The cousins did as they were told, and Lizzie kept her gun trained on them.

Amber turned her attention back to us. "So still sticking to your story?"

I looked at Victor.

"You're on your own, Stilts," he said, shaking his head. "I warned you."

I stayed quiet for a moment. This investigating thing had started out as a bit of a lark, a way to occupy some time and help some people. Make a little money, too. I had fallen into it, but I had stayed in it by choice. But I hadn't really considered it dangerous.

I was sitting in an abandoned house now, though, and people were armed. It wasn't comfortable, and I felt grossly underprepared and ill equipped. This wasn't what I'd envisioned, and to say I wasn't scared would be a big, fat lie. I didn't care if it was sorority girls aiming guns at me.

Guns were guns, and I didn't like being on the wrong end of them.

So I decided not to screw around.

"We came here to help Moe," I said. "That's the reason I contacted you in the first place."

Amber nodded excitedly, like there was going to be an exciting ending to the story.

"We were hired to find him," I said.

"You," Victor said. "You were hired."

"So you're, like, private eyes or something?" Amber asked, looking at each of us.

"Yep," I said.

"I've never met a private eye before," she said, smiling.

Her happy-go-lucky demeanor was unnerving.

"So that's why we're here," I said. "We were hired to find him and the money he stole."

She frowned. "Stole?"

"Yeah. To cover what I'm assuming he owed you."

She thought for a moment. "Well, he does owe us. But he's being totally difficult about it, ya know?"

"Actually, I don't," I said. "You wanna fill me in?"

She tilted her head and grinned, like I was some sort of puppy dog behind a glass window. "Well, we'll see about that. So the money you wanted to bet? It's not his?"

I shook my head. "Nope. I don't have that kind of money."

"Bummer," she said, making a face. "That would've made this so much easier." She tapped her chin with her finger. "Do you have any idea where our other things are?"

"Things?"

"The little blue pills," she said, raising an eyebrow.

"Ah. No. I have no idea where they are. I don't know what he did with the trophies."

Amber's face screwed up with confusion. "Trophies?"

"The soccer trophies that he was using to move them," I said. "He took the trophies from the same soccer association he stole the money from."

Amber stared at me for a moment, and the smile and goodwill melted away from her expression and body. "Soccer association?"

I wasn't sure what was happening, but I nodded.

She stood, descended the stairs, and faced the Huber cousins. Suzie came up next to her, and her normally surly demeanor had hardened even more.

"You stole from a soccer association?" Amber asked, her face a mixture of disgust and anger.

Neither Huber said anything.

She looked up at me. "Kids?"

"Yeah, it's a youth soccer group," I said.

"Oh my God!" she said. "That is unbelievable. How could you?"

The other sorority sisters whispered in agreement.

"You stole money *and* trophies from a bunch of kids?" Amber asked.

Neither Moises nor Elliott moved. She looked at me. I nodded.

Amber reached out and took the gun from Lizzie and pointed it right at Moe's forehead. "I'm gonna kill you."

47

Suzie reached out and gently pushed the barrel of the gun away from Moe's forehead. "No."

Amber looked at her, incredulous, stomping her foot on the porch. "He stole from a bunch of kids!" She looked at Moe. "You're a huge dick!"

Moe's shoulders were slumped, and I felt confident that he'd peed his pants.

"We're not shooting him," Suzie said.

"Why not?" Amber shouted. "I don't care if he owes us money. You don't steal from kids. Especially soccer kids. Oh my God, I hate you."

Moe leaned into his cousin, trying to increase his distance from her.

"I don't care," Suzie said. She took the gun from her. "Go cool off." Suzie nodded at Lizzie. "Take her inside. Get her something to drink."

Amber stepped back, swung her leg, and drilled Moe right in the shin. Moe fell off the step and toppled into the grass, grabbing at his leg.

"You are a *dick,*" she yelled at him as Lizzie escorted her into the house. "Their trophies, too? Dick!"

Suzie motioned for one of the other girls to cover the Hubers and came back up on the porch with us. She sat down in the chair Amber had been in.

"Amber used to play soccer," she said. "Actually, all of us did. So, uh, yeah, that didn't go over so well."

"Clearly."

Suzie leaned back in her chair and sighed. "Such a mess."

I agreed. It was a mess, and I still didn't understand most of it. But I felt like Amber's reaction had opened a window of opportunity. Maybe I could be an ally rather than an adversary.

"It's my daughter's soccer association," I said. "That's how I got brought into this."

"Did he steal everything?"

"Yeah. Games are going to be canceled this weekend," I said. "It's literally bankrupt."

"Jesus, she's gonna freak," Suzie whispered. "Freak."

"Did he pay you?" I asked. "Did he give you the money?"

She shook her head. "No. That's why the idiot is here."

Victor leaned forward. "He hasn't paid you anything?"

"No. Nothing. He tried to get cute."

"Cute?"

She started to say something, then stopped, her mouth closing shut. I could tell she was trying to decide how much to tell us. I didn't want her to shut down, didn't want that window of opportunity to close.

"Look," I said, "we don't care what you guys are running here. Honestly. We don't care. But I don't wanna see anyone get hurt here, and I really want my daughter to keep playing soccer."

She bit her bottom lip, working over what I'd told her. I didn't say anything else, because I didn't want to interrupt her thought process.

"He wanted us to cover what his cousin stole," she finally said quietly. "We forgave the debt in exchange for him picking up the Viagra. All he had to do was deliver and he was free and clear."

"I'm not following," I said.

"The betting, it makes us money," she said. "But the Viagra? You have any idea how much college boys will pay for that stuff?"

"Uh, no."

"A lot," she said. "A lot. No doctors, no prescriptions, no chance of public embarrassment. It's more popular than weed right now. Trust me."

I looked at Victor. He just shrugged and rolled his eyes.

"So those pills are worth a lot more to us," she said. "We knew we probably wouldn't see everything he owed us, so we just wanted to be done with him." She glanced at him. "But then he decided he'd hold the load hostage until we forked over enough cash for his cousin to return whatever he took from the casino." She shook her head. "Idiots."

I agreed with her assessment. They were very clearly idiots.

"So if you get the pills, this is over?" Victor asked.

"Absolutely," she said. "We don't want him or need him. I am tired of him. I want those pills before we hit the weekend. That's our busiest transaction time, and we've got people waiting."

College sure had changed since I'd been at A&M.

"Let us talk to him," Victor said. "Alone. Without the guns in his face."

"No way," she said. "You guys run out of here, we lose our money and our pills, and then it will get ugly."

Victor held out his keys. "We ain't going anywhere. Go inside. You can watch through the windows. We'll stay right here in the yard."

She chewed on her lip again. "Will he tell you?"

"Yeah," Victor said, glancing in Moe's direction. "He'll tell us."

"What happens if he doesn't?" she asked.

"Let's worry about that if we get there," Victor said. "But we aren't going anywhere, and we aren't denying he owes you. We're trying to help you get what you want. What do you have to lose?"

She studied each of us for a moment, then stood. "Ladies. In the house. Now."

The girls moved immediately and filed past us into the house.

"Take all the time you need," Suzie said. "I'll try to keep Amber at bay."

She disappeared inside.

The backyard now seemed quieter with fewer people.

"How do you know he's gonna tell us where the trophies are?" I asked.

Victor was rolling up his sleeves. "Because I'm going to beat his ass if he doesn't."

48

Moises Huber was still in the grass, clutching at his shin, as Victor bounded down the stairs.

"Get up, moron," Victor growled.

"Hey, he's hurt," Elliott said.

"And you just sit there and keep looking stupid," Victor barked, pointing at him. "I blame you for us even being here."

"And what the hell are you doing here, anyway?" I asked.

Elliott shifted his eyes to the ground. "I followed you."

"Here?"

"As soon as you went in the house, a couple of those girls came out of nowhere and pulled me out of my car," he said, shaking his head.

"Now I'm really pissed at you," Victor said. "For following me." He looked down at Moises. "You got five seconds to get up, before I start kicking you in the shins *and* the nuts."

Moises pushed himself to his knees and crawled over to the stairs, dirt and grass clinging to the back of his shirt and hair. He got himself up and sat next to his cousin.

Victor rubbed his hands together. "Here's how it's gonna go, boys. Deuce and I have a few questions for you. You're going to answer them. Honestly. If you don't, those crazy chicks are gonna come back out here and shoot you. And we're not gonna stop them."

"But you can't just . . . ," Moises protested.

"Shut up!" Victor yelled at him. "I didn't ask you any questions yet, and the only time I want either of you to open your stupid mouths is if one of us asks you a question. Because I am pissed off that I'm wasting a day in some godforsaken crap hole with you two idiots and a bunch of nutty broads waving guns around in my face. And right now I'd just as soon they come back out here and start taking target practice. It makes no difference to me."

I had to hand it to him. They were rock still, with both their mouths closed. He had their attention. He was one scary-ass midget.

Victor looked at me. "Now, because I don't understand any of this lunacy, you start asking whatever the hell you need to ask so we can get outta this place."

"Where are the trophies, Moe?" I asked.

"I'm not telling," he said, shaking his head.

Victor growled and started for him, but I put a hand on his chest and held him back.

"I swear I will rip his legs off," Victor said. "This is ridiculous."

"Just hang on," I said to him.

He knocked my hand away but didn't go any closer to Moe.

"You tell me where the trophies are and all of this goes away," I said. "All of it. That's all they want."

"It doesn't go away," Moe insisted. "My cousin still owes the casino. I still owe Rose Petal soccer."

"And the church," I said. "Don't forget that."

He looked at me, confused, but then just shook his head. "None of it really goes away."

"How about the fact that they won't shoot you?" I asked. "How about that?"

He didn't have an answer for me.

"Just tell them," Elliott said. "I'll figure out my own problems."

"No," Moe said. "You did it to help me. I'm not gonna leave you hanging like that."

"You got, like, three minutes to tell us where the trophies are, before I tell them to load up," Victor snarled. "I am *done* with this."

"Look," I said, "you are just making this worse by keeping their stuff. They are willing to wash your debt. But you gotta give them the Viagra. It's not negotiable."

"And then what happens?" Moe said. "So they let us go. Then what? Jail?"

"Probably," I admitted. "But that's probably better than getting shot, isn't it? Because I'm pretty sure they will shoot you."

Actually, I was starting to think they wouldn't. Suzie seemed exhausted by the entire thing and just wanted to move on. The way she'd moved the gun away from Amber indicated to me that she didn't want anyone getting shot.

But it was okay if Moe hadn't picked up on that.

"Fine," Moe finally said.

"Yippee skippee," Victor said, throwing his hands up.

"But I'm going to get them," Moe said. "I have to be the one to get them."

"Why you?" I asked.

"Because that's the deal," Moe said. "They can shoot me if they don't like it."

"This guy's unbelievable," Victor said. "Can we just go in and tell them to shoot him? I'll buy lunch."

I wasn't sure what Moe was angling for, but we were at least headed in the right direction, and I didn't want it to stall out.

"Stay here," I said to Victor.

"BBQ, burgers, I don't care," Victor said. "You choose. I'll buy."

Suzie was watching from the window, and I motioned for her to come out. I met her on the porch.

"Did he tell you?" she asked, her eyes hopeful.

"Not exactly," I said and told her his proposition.

She shook her head. "No way. He'll take off. I know it. He's such a weasel."

"What if I go with him?" I said. "I guarantee you I'll bring him and the Viagra back to you."

"I don't exactly trust you," she said. "You've been lying to us for a couple days now."

She had me there.

"I lied to you to figure out what was going on," I said. "I will bring him back to you. You want collateral of some sort? Wallet? Driver's license? My home address? I'll give it to you. I'll bring him back."

"Hang on a sec," she said and disappeared back into the house.

"You tell them to get bigger guns?" Victor hollered. "So they don't miss?"

I held up a finger, telling him to hold on.

Victor held up his middle finger, telling me to . . . you know.

Thirty seconds later Suzie came back out with a decidedly calmer Amber.

"You'll take him and bring him back?" Amber said. "With the Viagra?"

"Yep. Guaranteed."

"Okay," she said, nodding. "But the cousin stays."

I didn't see any problem with that. "That works."

"And so does the midget," she said, a smile finding its way back onto her face.

"Victor? Why?"

"Megan's coming over," she said. "She'll be thrilled to see him again."

I turned back to the yard. Victor stood there, arms folded across his chest, frowning at me.

"I can't make him stay," I said to Amber.

"You're going to have to," she said, raising an eyebrow. "That's the deal."

I thought for a moment. I didn't think she really had that much leverage, because, in truth, they needed the Viagra. I felt like we could wait them out and they'd eventually cave, because they needed it more than we needed anything else.

But they also had the guns.

"Okay," I said. "But play along with me for a minute, all right?"

She nodded.

"Moe," I said, turning to the yard. "Come here."

Moe took a few moments before he moved tentatively in my direction. He trudged up the steps to the porch.

"Go inside with her," I said quietly to him, nodding at Suzie. "Wait for me."

Suzie didn't wait for a response. She took him by the arm and escorted him into the house.

I hopped down the steps into the yard and motioned Victor away from Elliott.

"Can I have the keys to your car?" I said. "I left my phone in there, and I wanna record the conversation inside."

Victor dug in his pocket. "What conversation?"

"He's gonna give up the location," I lied. "I want it on tape."

He pulled out the keys and handed them to me. "And then can we get the hell outta here?"

"Absolutely," I said, wondering how pissed he was going to be at me. "Keep an eye on this one, all right? We don't need him doing anything stupid when we're finishing this."

"Roger," he said, frowning around me at Elliott.

I turned back to the house and hopped up the stairs.

"You're probably gonna need some help containing him," I whispered, "when he realizes . . ."

"Hey, why do you need my keys when the top is down?" Victor yelled.

". . . that I'm leaving him here," I finished, continuing past her toward the house.

"Deuce?" Victor yelled, louder now. "What are you doing?"

Amber whistled loudly, and several of her sorority sisters shuffled outside, guns at the ready.

"Deuce! What's going on?"

I turned at the door. "I'll be back as soon as I can. You'll be fine."

Pure, unfiltered anger filled every molecule of his face, and he charged toward the porch. The girls quickly closed in on him and corralled him as he swung and kicked in every imaginable way, spitting and cursing in my direction.

It appeared as if he was going to be very pissed at me.

49

"You have caused me quite a few headaches," I said.

"I'm sure," Moe said, leaning back in the passenger seat. "I'm sorry."

I'd put the top up on Victor's Miata and unstrapped the blocks from the pedals, but I could still hear him screaming at me from the other side of the house.

I almost felt bad.

Moe and I were on the highway, headed north of Dallas, and he still hadn't given me the exact location of where we were going yet. I was trying to be patient and engage him in conversation to pass the time.

"How did all this start?" I asked.

He laughed an empty laugh. "Probably a football pool when I was a kid. I could pick winners every week. I'd play against my dad, and I'd win ten bucks each week. I liked it."

I didn't intend for him to give me his life history,

but now that he was talking, I didn't want to stop him, either.

"So . . . since then," he said, shrugging, "I've learned more, figured out how to do it smartly, figured out which games gave me good odds, learned lots of the tricks, and . . ." He shrugged again. "I don't know. It just grew."

"How did you hook up with the sorority?" I asked.

"Anybody who lays money in Dallas knows about them," he said. "It's not a secret. They were easy to find. And weird as it sounds, they have a good rep. They play fair." He glanced at me. "This really is all my fault."

"How so?"

"I gambled money I didn't have," he said. "Cardinal sin. Don't lay money you don't have. But I got cocky and thought I had sure things going."

"But you didn't."

He shook his head and shifted in the seat. "I couldn't win a thing. Dry spell to end all dry spells. Everything I touched turned to crap. I just kept thinking it was going to turn. And I kept betting bigger to cover the losses."

"And the losses just grew."

Moe nodded. "Yep. Like a snowball in a hurry. I finally had to tell them I couldn't cover."

"How'd that go?"

"They gave me some time to cover, but it was too much," he said. "I knew it was too much, and they probably did, too, but I think they were trying to give me an out to come up with something. Then I panicked and stole the money from the soccer association."

"Did they threaten you?" I asked, switching lanes. "Is that why you panicked?"

"Not really," he said. "I'd just never been under like that, and I freaked out. I just made it worse."

That was an understatement.

"So I stole the money, but it wasn't enough," he continued. "Elliott knew I was in over my head. He said he'd help if I'd quit gambling. I promised him I would."

"You mean it?"

He glanced at me. "Absolutely. But then I felt guilty that he took the money from his casino. I'd just made it worse for him, too."

I didn't say anything.

"But I was still short," he said. "I gave them what I had, but I was still short. So they offered me the Viagra deal. Seemed easy enough, and it was. But then, when I was coming back, I just felt bad for my cousin. I got mad, frustrated, whatever. I didn't want him to suffer for my screwup. So I came up with the idea to have them pay him back what he'd stolen for me."

It literally made no sense, but I assumed the anxiety and fear made it all perfectly clear to him at the time. Every time Moe dug a hole, he kept digging a bigger one to bury himself in.

"They obviously didn't like that," he said, frowning. "So here we are."

"Okay, here's what I don't get," I said, trying to add everything up. "You took the soccer money and your cousin's money and the church's money. How was that not enough?"

"Church money?" he asked.

"I talked to Haygood," I said. "He told me you took money from them, as well."

I sensed a change in his body language and demeanor but couldn't figure out exactly what it meant.

"I didn't steal from the church," he finally said.

"He says you did, and it was a pretty hefty chunk of change."

"I didn't steal from the church," he said a little louder, agitated. "If I had, I wouldn't have needed to do the Viagra run. I would've had enough to pay them what I owed them."

"Then why did he tell me you took their money?" I asked.

He shifted in the seat again, and the sad sack that I'd seen for the last couple hours was gone. Moises Huber was now one irritated dude.

"Because Haygood is the biggest liar alive."

50

Moe directed me off the freeway when we got north of the suburbs and pointed me in the direction of Applegate Lake.

"Okay," I said. "You're gonna need to explain that statement about Haygood."

I glanced over at him, and his face was tight with anger.

"If that guy told me the sky was blue, I wouldn't believe it," he said. "He's incredible. He says I took the money?"

I recounted my conversation with the pastor.

He shook his head. "I don't know why I'm surprised." He stared at the window for a moment. "Look, I know I'm an easy target to blame things on. I don't think my . . . issues . . . are any secret. But I've never taken a penny from that church. Not a single cent."

He seemed genuine, but I wasn't exactly batting a thousand with my perceptive senses. "Then why does he say you took it?"

"Because, like I said, I'm an easy target," he said. "He took it."

"Haygood?"

He nodded. "Ever since I've been there, he's been shady with money. Because it's a religious institution and gets all sorts of tax breaks, there isn't a lot of oversight outside of the church." He paused. "Know where he lives?"

"No."

"Out on the lake west of Rose Petal," he said. "House is about seven thousand square feet. Probably worth about five million."

I couldn't hide my surprise. "Wow."

He chuckled and shook his head. "Right? Drives this ridiculous Mercedes every day. Wife drives a bright orange Hummer. And everything that guy spends comes out of the church coffers. Everything."

"How is that possible?"

"No oversight," Moe said. "Except in house. Us. And he tells us how to handle it all. He travels in private jets, stays only in five-star hotels, shops at the most expensive stores. And all of that is funded by the donations of the people who roll into the church every weekend. All of it. He doesn't pay himself a salary. He just takes what he wants."

I wasn't exactly sure what I thought a church pastor should earn, but I certainly didn't think it was a salary that could afford all those things that Moe was telling me about. And I really didn't think the money that went into the basket during services should be used to fund his closet. That seemed . . . not good.

"Okay," I said. "So he's playing with the money. And I don't know the rules regarding church and spending. But then why would he need to steal and blame it on you if he's already essentially living on the money that comes into the church?"

Moe shook his head. "You'll see. Take a right up here."

I turned where he instructed. "I'll see?"

He nodded but didn't say anything else.

The road was barren at first, just a path through empty fields and forgotten fences. But then properties started showing up. Small houses on oversize lots first, then the houses grew in stature the closer we got to the lake, as did the lot size. Mansions started showing up on rolling acres, new money trying to pretend like they were people of the country.

He directed me through a maze of roads, then told me to pull over in what looked like the middle of nowhere.

"We should walk from here," he said. "I'm not sure if anyone's out here. Probably not, but we should be careful."

"Careful of what?"

"Careful that Haygood's not here."

"We're at Haygood's house?"

He smiled. "One of them, yeah."

I shook my head and got out.

We walked up the road, following a carefully constructed and maintained split rail fence painted white. It looked like a massive horse property. After a couple hundred yards, we came to a gate and Moe threw himself over it.

"We aren't gonna get shot, are we?" I asked.

He shook his head. "He doesn't believe in guns. And I doubt he's here. He's almost never here."

I hesitated, reminded myself that I needed to quit this job, then jumped over the fence.

"He sent me out here one time," Moe said as we walked along a gravel path. "Needed me to pick something up from the house. He told me not to tell anyone about it. Because he didn't want anyone getting jealous." He shook his head. "In reality, he just doesn't want anyone to know what he does with the money he takes."

"So did he take the money to pay for this?" I asked, still not getting it.

He shook his head. "Oh, no. This is paid for. I saw the deed. Free and clear."

Maybe I needed to move from private investigating to church pastoring.

"So then why did he take it?" I asked.

"You'll see," he said again.

I was getting a bit exasperated but tried to remind myself that we were getting closer to the end of all this crap. Or at least I hoped so.

Another hundred yards and what I at first thought was a house started to emerge from behind a rolling, grassy hillside. As we got closer, though, I realized it was a barn. A barn the size of a mansion.

"He doesn't even keep horses," Moe said. "He just wanted some massive, oversize property."

"The maintenance alone must be killer," I said.

"About a hundred grand a month," he said, without missing a beat. He glanced at me. "I pay the bill."

"He's really that brazen?"

"There isn't a single person working in the financial department at the church that doesn't know this is how he lives and operates," he said. "They may not know about every single thing. Like I'm not sure who knows about this place. But I'm sure there are things I don't know about. He's smart. He spreads it around so it looks like less."

I nodded.

The barn was about three stories high, painted a light beige with white trim. There was a bank of windows on the top level and massive doors at the front, big enough to drive a motor home through.

Or a twenty-five-foot U-Haul.

There was a combo lock on the doors, and Moe took it in his hands and spun the dial back and forth. It popped open.

"He never uses this," he said. "He doesn't even know the combo. I bought the lock."

He unclasped the lock and pulled hard on one of the doors, which was twice his size. He backpedaled as he pulled it open. He got it flush against the side of the barn and attached it to a metal loop so it would stay open.

I stepped into the dark interior, and it took my eyes a moment to adjust to the dark. When they did, I saw a massive U-Haul.

And a Porsche.

"The U-Haul is mine," he said. "Trophies are in the back." He paused. "The Porsche is hers."

"Hers?"

"Yeah. Hers. His mistress."

51

"I'm not sure anyone else knows about her," Moe said. "And I think he told me only because he felt like he had leverage on me."

"Leverage?" I asked.

"My gambling," he said, and he seemed to physically shrink again when he said it. It might have been his addiction, but he clearly wasn't proud of it. "He'd made it clear he knew that I had a problem."

"How did he know?"

"Again, most everyone knows I gamble. But I always got the sense that he knew more. Who knows?" He shrugged. "The guy's a weasel."

Clearly.

"So he would make these sort of veiled threats that if I ever opened my mouth, he'd somehow use it against me," he said. "I'm not exactly sure how he could, but I've been so nervous about the money I owed, I wasn't thinking clearly. I just let him bully me."

I didn't want to feel badly for Moe. And most of me didn't. Most of what he was tied up in was his own doing, and there was nothing that could convince me that stealing would ever be okay.

But there was a sincerity to his remorse that made me think he really was sorry. And the picture he was painting of Haygood made me dislike Haygood far more than Moe. Maybe that wasn't fair, but that was the way it was shaping up for me.

"Anyway," Moe continued, messing with the lock on the back of the U-Haul. "He got stuck in a meeting, and she needed a ride from the airport. I was working late in my office. He told me to go pick her up and to not tell anyone and we'd talk about it the next day. So I did."

I leaned against the Porsche, listening.

"She's real nice," he said. "Very friendly, pretty. Not sure how they met. I didn't ask a lot of questions. She asked me to bring her here, and I guess she lives here most of the time."

He popped the lock on the back of the truck and set it on the bumper. "That was the first time I'd ever been here. I dropped her here and then went back to the office. He was waiting for me. He didn't try to spin who she was. He was pretty clear about it. And he was also clear that I wasn't to say anything, or I'd lose my job, and again, he made some veiled threats about my gambling." He frowned. "And I just went along with it."

"When was this?"

"About six months ago," he said. "So then, after I knew, I guess he decided he could use me. So I pick her up at the airport when she's in town, help her out if she needs anything, that kind of thing. He can keep his distance from her." He smiled. "Except when he doesn't."

"So does he just tell you when to go get her?"

He shook his head. "Nah. We set up a way to send messages. On Facebook."

I thought back to when Victor suggested I check out his account. "MacDonald."

Surprise rose in his face. "Yeah. How'd you know?"

"I just took a look at your page. It was the one thing that stuck out to me before you disappeared. I didn't know who it was, though. Just one of those loose end things."

He raised an eyebrow. "Man, he'd freak if he thought anyone picked up on anything. He lives in fear of his wife finding out."

"I'll bet."

"So after I decided to hang on to the trophies, this was the one place I knew I could hide them." His mouth twisted sourly. "She's out of town, he rarely comes out here, it's big enough, and no one knows about it. I knew it would be safe."

I nodded. It was a pretty good hiding place. If you needed to hide kids soccer trophies filled with Viagra.

He swung the door to the truck open. Stacks of rectangular boxes filled nearly the entire interior.

"Took me ninety minutes to load the truck," he said. "In the middle of the night."

"Belinda said that's probably when you did it."

He sighed loudly and slumped on the truck's bumper. "She must hate me."

I didn't say anything.

"Everyone must hate me," he said. "I hate me. I'm so stupid. This whole thing is so stupid. I'm gonna lose my job, probably go to jail."

I felt sorry for him. I didn't want to, but I did.

"I know a lawyer," I said. "She can help you."

"Who's gonna wanna help me? Why would they?"

I thought of his gambling problem and the addiction and the fact that he hadn't harmed anyone. And that he was fessing up. I hoped that Julianne would be able to do something with that.

"She will help you if she can," I told him. "She's good. The best."

"I can't pay her."

"We'll figure it out." I motioned at the truck. "Let's get this thing back out so we can get back and get your cousin and my partner."

"Not so fast," a voice said behind me.

52

The guy on the left in the barn entrance was unfamiliar, but I recognized his partner.

The guy who I'd tangled with at Comanche River.

And Myrtle Callaghan was standing between them.

"Who the hell are you?" Moe asked, immediately slamming the door on the U-Haul shut.

"Mr. Winters, nice to see you again," Callaghan said.

"If you say so," I said.

There was no love lost for me when it came to her and her casino flunkies. I was still irritated at the way I'd been treated there, and I didn't care what the reason was. The suite didn't make up for it, either. She was someone I'd hoped to never see again.

"You're Elliott's cousin, I presume?" she said, motioning at Moe.

"Why are you here?" I asked before he could answer. "Were you following us?"

"I told you we would find a way to recoup our money," she said. "One way or another."

"Way to not answer my question."

She ignored me and gestured for the suits to approach the truck. I heard the lock snap in place.

"There's no money in there," Moises said.

"We're gonna take a look, anyway," Myrtle said.

"There's no money in there," I said.

"Again," she said, "we'd like to take a look."

"You're problem isn't with us," I said. "It's with Elliott."

"Who isn't here at the moment."

The suits stopped when they reached me.

"Fine," I said to Moe. "Let 'em look."

"But . . ."

"There's no money in there," I said to Myrtle. "We let you have a look and you walk. Deal?"

"No deal."

"Really?" I looked at the suits. "Got any bolt cutters on you?"

They looked at each other, then at her.

She pursed her lips.

"Because I think we just forgot the combo," I said. "In fact, I'm positive we did."

Myrtle thought this over for a moment.

"We let you look," I said again. "And when there's no money in there, you walk away. And stay the hell off my tail."

"I'm not gonna promise that," she said. "I want my money back."

"You'll get it," I said.

I could feel Moises shift behind me, nervous.

"Really? You know where it is?" she asked, raising an eyebrow.

"You'll get your money," I said. "I'm working on it."

"So you'll vouch for it?" she said. "You'll take responsibility for it?"

I didn't like the way she said that, but I had to put my money—or hers—where my mouth was.

"Yeah," I said. "I'll vouch for it."

She stared at me for a moment, then nodded. "Deal. Open it."

I looked at Moises. "Let 'em look."

He looked at me, totally bewildered.

"Just do it," I said. "It'll be fine."

He shook his head, confused, but dialed the combo on the lock. He pulled it off, opened up the doors, and stepped to the side.

The suits rushed past us and climbed up into the truck. They immediately started ripping boxes open. After a minute, the one I'd wrestled with looked back at his boss in frustration.

"There's nothing here but a bunch of kids soccer trophies," he told her.

He held one up for good measure.

The trophies were about six inches high, an oversize metal soccer ball perched on a wooden platform. ROSE PETAL SOCCER was engraved on the platform.

Myrtle approached the truck and held her hand out. The suit handed her the trophy. She spun it around in her hands, shook it, stared at it.

It remained a trophy.

She handed it back to the suit and stared at me. "All right. You win."

"Hardly."

"Exactly," she said, nodding. "You're on the hook now."

"I'll live."

"If you say so," she said. "But a deal's a deal."

I tried not to let out an audible breath.

"When will I see my money?" she asked.

"Soon."

"I want a date."

"That wasn't part of the deal," I said. "And I'm happily married."

She gave me an icy look that told me she couldn't take a joke, and that made me worry about my sperm count.

"Soon," I said seriously.

She folded her arms across her chest. "All right. Soon. But I won't wait long." She lifted her chin at the suits. "Let's go."

The one I didn't know jumped down first. My pal was next, and I managed to hip check him just before he hit the ground. He fell to his right and tumbled onto the dirt floor.

"Oh," I said. "Sorry."

He bounced up, his face red, his fists balled up.

"Teddy," Myrtle said. "Leave it alone. We're leaving."

He looked from her to me and back to her.

"Now," she commanded.

He reluctantly unclenched his fists and dusted himself off.

"We'll see you," Myrtle said, backing up, heading for the barn entrance. "Soon."

I hoped so.

53

"How exactly are you going to pay them?" Moises asked.

We'd backed the truck up out of the barn, and he'd just finished relocking it.

"I'm working on it," I said.

"You heard those girls," he said, irritated. "They aren't going to cover it. That's why I hid this stuff in the first place!"

"I know that."

"And that chick was crazy enough to follow us out here, and I don't think she's gonna forget that you told her she'd get her money soon."

"I know that."

"So what are you going to do?" Moe demanded. "How are you going to get her that money?"

"I told you," I said. "I'm working on it."

"How? By planning a bank robbery?"

"Have I so far managed to keep your butt safe today?" I asked him. "Have I screwed anything up yet for you today? Or have I managed to keep everyone who's pissed at you from kicking your ass?"

He shrunk again but didn't say anything.

"Exactly," I said. "And I don't have any plans to screw it up now. So maybe, just maybe, you should let me run the show here and trust me."

His head hung like a dog that just peed on the new carpeting. "Okay. I just don't get why you wanna help me."

Truth was, I didn't know, either. I did think he was sorry for the mess that he'd created, but this really was all of his own making. He'd made the decisions, and now the consequences were surrounding him like alligators.

But there was something vulnerable about him that was making me soften toward him. I didn't like the people around him, either, and part of me felt like they had all preyed on a guy who was easy to prey on. And that didn't feel right to me, either.

Moe climbed into the driver's seat of the U-Haul, and I walked around to the passenger side. He was gonna drive me out to the edge of the property and then we'd grab my car and he'd follow me back to the house to make the exchange.

But I wasn't lying to him.

Coming out to this property and listening to the things he'd told me about Haygood got me thinking.

And for some foolish reason, I started thinking I could come up with a plan to solve everybody's problems and minimize the damage.

That was probably why Julianne often told me I shouldn't do so much thinking.

54

Victor was still screaming when we got back to the ramshackle house.

"Oh, great!" he shouted when I walked through the door. "You did decide to come back. What a treat for all of us."

"Good to see you haven't been harmed," I said.

He was sitting on a ratty-looking couch between Amber and Megan. Megan's arm was looped through his. Elliott was sitting across from them, scrunched down in a torn-up easy chair. The other girls were spread out around the living room floor, guns either at their sides or in their laps.

Just another normal afternoon at the sorority house.

"I could've been!" he shouted. "You gargantuan traitor!"

"Has he been like this the entire time?" I asked Amber.

"Oh, pretty much," she said, chomping on a piece of gum. "But it's, like, you know, kinda cute."

"Really? Cute?"

"Oh, totes," she said, nodding and chomping.

"Mmm-hmm," Megan purred.

"You and I are gonna have a serious talk when we get outta here," he said, his eyes narrowed.

I didn't doubt that. I really couldn't blame him. I'd absolutely hung him out to dry, and if he'd done the same thing to me, I would've been furious. Somehow, though, I didn't think the girls would've found me as charming.

But we could argue that later.

"The truck is outside," I said.

Amber jumped up and started clapping her hands. "Yay!"

Suzie scrambled to her feet and headed out to inspect it. She was back in thirty seconds.

"It's locked," she said. "Combo?"

"I wanna talk to Amber first," I said. "Alone."

"I'm gonna tell your wife," Victor spat.

"And I'm gonna tell yours that you spent the entire afternoon holding hands with Megan."

He quickly disentangled himself from a disappointed Megan. "You wouldn't."

"Close your trap and I won't have to."

He let out something akin to a growl but didn't say anything.

"I want the combo," Suzie said. "Now. That stuff is ours, and I wanna see that it's there."

"It's there," I said. "All of it. But I wanna talk to Amber first. Out back."

All the girls perked up a bit, and tension rippled through the room, as they clearly thought I was trying to pull something over on them.

"Bring a gun," I said. "I just wanna talk. I'll give you the combo after we're done. Promise."

Amber shrugged. "Cool. Come on."

Annoyance crept over Suzie's face, but she didn't say anything.

"Try not to leave me and steal my car again," Victor grumbled.

"I won't," I assured him.

He made a face at me.

Amber grabbed a handgun off the floor. "Just in case."

I followed her out the back door, and she hopped down the stairs and into the grass. "Okay. What's up?"

"I wasn't lying," I said. "All the trophies are in there with the Viagra. They were right where Moises said they were."

"Sweet!" she said, grinning. "That's totally gonna make everyone so happy, and we won't have to shoot anyone today! Those are always good days!"

I momentarily wondered about the days they did have to shoot people, but quickly swept it aside.

"So Moises is good with you, then, right?" I asked.

She thought, then nodded. "Yeppers. I'm still pissed at him for stealing from those soccer kids, but I think it's totally good if we just go our separate ways now."

"I agree," I said.

"And we totally will give you the trophies," she said. "We can unpack 'em and just keep the little blue pills." She giggled. "But the trophies are yours. I don't want the kids to not get 'em."

"Let's talk about the kids for a second," I said.

She wrinkled her nose, confused.

"I can give them the trophies," I said. "But I can't give them their season."

"Totally not comprehending."

"The money that Moises stole to pay you—it belonged to them."

"I know, silly. You already told us that. Huge bummer."

"I mean, not only is their season done, but the entire association is probably gonna close. They won't be able to operate anymore."

"Seriously," she said, frowning, "that just sucks."

"I agree. It does suck. So I'm wondering if you could help me out."

She wrinkled her nose again.

"I want you to help," I said.

"How?"

"I want you to make a donation to the association," I said. "So we can play games this weekend and keep it afloat."

"Do you guys play on, like, water?"

"It's an expression. It means to keep it running."

"Ohhhh."

"Yeah."

She chomped on the gun for a minute. "How much?"

"Seventy-three thousand dollars."

Her eyes bulged, and she burst into laughter. "That's funny!"

"I'm serious."

"Oh my God, I might pee my pants. You're hilarious."

"I'm not kidding, Amber. I want you to do this."

She stopped laughing and looked at me like I was crazy. "You want us to just give them the money?"

"I saw how mad you got when you learned that he

took the money from the soccer association," I said. "You know it's not right."

"Well, duh."

"And they have no way to get that money back. Their bank account right now is completely empty. Every kid in Rose Petal is going to be crying this weekend, when I go back and tell them that we can't rent the fields and that we can't pay for the referees."

Her lips tightened. "Can't you do, like, a fund-raiser or something?"

"By Saturday? Uh, no."

She nodded, realizing that wasn't possible.

"They need the money," I said. "And you have it. I'm willing to bet that seventy-three thousand is a drop in the bucket for you guys right now. Right?"

"Oh, I don't do the money," she said. "Megan does."

"Call her out here."

She turned to the house. "Megan!"

Ten seconds later Megan emerged on the porch. "What?"

"Come here."

Megan trudged down the steps. "The little man is being mean."

"He's always mean," I said.

"I don't believe that."

"Trust me."

"Megan, do we have, like, a ton of money in our accounts?" Amber asked, hands on her hips.

Megan glanced at me, then at Amber. "Why?"

"Cuz I wanna know."

Megan started to say something, then leaned in closer to Amber, cupped her hand around her mouth, and whispered into Amber's ear.

Amber's eyes went huge, and she punched Megan in the shoulder. "Shut! Up!"

"Ouch!"

"We have that much!"

Megan rubbed her shoulder and nodded.

"Oh my God, you're like the best treasurer ever!" Amber said, then wrapped her arms around Megan tightly.

Megan stood there stiffly, unsure what to do.

Amber let her loose. "Okay. You can go back in. Thanks!"

Megan headed back up the stairs and disappeared into the house.

"I take it you guys are doing okay," I said.

"Uh, yeah!" Amber said, looking like she was about ready to break into a clapping fit again. "I am so not good at math, but thank God Megan is, because whatever she is doing, it is totally working! We are, like, rich!"

"That's good to hear," I said. "So you can donate the money."

Her enthusiasm waned. "I dunno. It feels like we're just giving him his money back, and that's a total no-no."

"He's not going to be running the soccer programs anymore," I said. "That's a guarantee."

"For sure?"

"For sure. There's a woman named Belinda who I think will probably be in charge."

"Oh, I love the name Belinda!"

"Uh, sure. Okay."

"So we would be giving her the money, then? Not him?"

"You'd be giving it to the association, but she'd be

the one managing it," I assured her. "And honestly, Amber. It's their money. They shouldn't suffer because Moises has a gambling problem. That isn't fair. It's not fair to my daughter and all the other kids."

"But we didn't take it from them. He did."

"I know that," I said, feeling like I had her close. "But this is a chance to do the right thing."

She chewed on a fingernail. "What if I say no?"

I pretended to think on that for a moment. "Well, there's not much I can do, really. I promised you the Viagra, and I'm giving it to you. Probably the only thing I could do is to tell the people in Rose Petal that the soccer season is over because Moises gambled away all the money with you guys and now—"

"Whoa," she said, concerned. "Whoa. You would tell them about us?"

"Well, I wouldn't use your names, but it sounds like most everyone would know who you are. Do you get a lot of clients from Rose Petal?" I asked.

"Like, a ton, yeah."

"Oh. Well, that might not sit so well with the parents. They might want to take their business elsewhere. But who knows?"

Amber stuck her index finger and thumb in her mouth and ripped off an ear-shattering whistle. Suzie and Megan materialized on the porch in seconds.

"Meeting," Amber said, waving them down. "Right now."

She escorted them over to the corner of the yard, where I couldn't hear them. It was like Amber transformed right in front of my eyes. She went from being the ditsy, gum-chewing face of the organization to the absolute leader in seconds. Her face was grim, and she was gesturing with her hands to her two sorority sisters, speaking emphatically. They were listening raptly. She moved her gaze from each of them, and then they both nodded.

All three came back over to me.

"Okay," Amber said. "You have a deal."

"Really?"

"For sure," she said, lapsing back into her dumb girl mode. "But you have to promise me that you'll talk us up, 'kay? Don't give us a bum rap, 'kay?" She paused. "I don't wanna have to come and shoot you!"

It was silent for a moment.

Then she dissolved into a fit of giggles.

55

It took an hour to unload the U-Haul, and the girls formed an assembly line to take the trophies apart, remove the Viagra, and put the trophies back together. They worked efficiently and had them all back together inside of another hour and the truck was reloaded and we were ready to go.

Moises and Elliott climbed into the cab of the truck, and I walked around to Moises's side.

"I'll call you later," I said. "Lay low. Maybe stay out with your cousin. I'm gonna try and work a few other things out."

"Like what?"

"Like let me worry about it," I said.

He started to say something, then caught himself and nodded. "Okay. Thank you."

"You're welcome," I said, then looked past him. "And so are you."

"Thank you," Elliott said unenthusiastically.

"You stay with him, too," I said. "I'm working on you, too."

Elliott shrugged and slumped in the seat.

I tapped the door. "I'll be in touch."

Moises nodded. I stepped down off the runner. He started the engine, and the truck pulled away slowly from the curb.

Victor was in the front yard, saying his good-byes to his new friends.

He'd mellowed a little bit.

"Ladies, thank you for your company," he said. "I appreciate your hospitality."

A surge of giggles rippled through the girls.

"I wish we could've met under different circumstances," he continued. "But should you ever need my assistance, you have my card."

They all nodded enthusiastically.

He adjusted his fedora and strutted past me to the car.

Amber joined me at the curb. "I'll get you a check tomorrow."

"That would be great. Thank you."

"You're welcome," she said. "I'll probably just stick it in your mailbox, if that's cool."

"You need my address?"

She grinned. "I know where you live."

I started to ask how, then decided against it.

"Toodles!" she said and wandered back to the gaggle of girls still eyeing Victor.

I slid into the seat next to him.

"I oughta leave your big dumb butt here," he said.

"You probably should," I said. "I'm sorry."

"Oh, you're gonna be sorry. Trust me on that."

"Still. I'm sorry. But I wanted to get this done."

"Well, thank God we are done with this crap," he said, shaking his head.

"Well, we sorta aren't."

He turned the key in the ignition. "Excuse me?"

"I learned some things while Moe and I were gone."

"So what? He's free, they got their stuff, and you got the trophies. Done."

"Not quite."

He revved the engine. The girls oohed and aahed on the lawn.

"Well, this oughta be real interesting."

"It is. And I need your help."

He stared at me like I'd lost my mind.

"I know, I know," I said. "You owe me, and I deserve it. But I seriously need your help to finish this off. To do the right thing."

"The right thing would be to punch you in the stomach."

"After, when we're done, you can punch me in the stomach."

He raised an eyebrow. "Yeah?"

I nodded. "Swear. Help me finish this, and you can have a free shot."

He revved the engine again, and we shot away from the curb, his cackle drowning out the engine.

56

The next morning there was a check in my mailbox, as promised.

I tried not to be creeped out by the fact that Amber knew where I lived without me telling her. I wasn't sure I'd ever understand the dichotomy they all presented between being airheaded sorority girls and ruthless gambling moguls.

I showed the check to Julianne.

She raised an eyebrow at me. "Nice work, Detective."

"I thought so."

"Did you have to sell your soul to get it?"

"Nope. Not even a little."

"Even more impressive."

"I might've promised your services to someone, though."

"Certainly you're joking."

I was exhausted when I had finally gotten home and had just given her the bare bones about what had transpired over the course of the day. I fell asleep before I even finished, so the entire conversation was foggy. But I knew I hadn't mentioned the offer I'd made to Moe.

I quickly told her what I'd said to him about legal representation.

She didn't roll her eyes at me, which was always a good sign.

"He has no intention of pretending he didn't do it?" she asked when I was done.

"No, don't think so. He really seems sorry that he did all of this."

"That'll help," she said. "Okay. I'll see what I can come up with for him. But if the soccer association doesn't file against him, he should be okay. It was his cousin that stole the money from the casino."

"I'm just guessing they'll have to file against him. To cover themselves financially."

"They can just remove him from the board," Julianne said. "With the check, they've got money for their operating costs now. They should be functional. So they probably don't have to unless they want to."

I remember how upset Belinda was initially and how she'd called him a weasel. It was hard for me to envision her being talked out of pressing charges against Moe.

"There would be costs associated with charging him," Julianne said, reading my mind. "Especially if they went after him in civil court. And they've made it clear they don't have the money to do anything like that. They can't even pay you."

So maybe Moe's future wasn't so bleak, after all. Maybe he could survive all of this and get some help to curb his gambling.

I held up the check. "I need to take this to Belinda."

Julianne set her coffee cup down and put her arms around my neck. "The child is still sleeping. I was hoping you might ravish me before she woke."

My skin tingled. "Oh."

Her lips brushed my neck. "We could be fast."

"I could, uh, manage that."

Her lips found my ear. "I missed you yesterday. And I still want a baby."

"Then I probably owe you."

"Yes. I'm certain you do. Particularly if you want me to help Moises."

"So would this be like an advance on services?"

She bit my earlobe. "It would be like the first in an installment plan."

"Do I need to sign something?"

She kept her arms around my neck and pulled me toward the stairs. "No. I know where you live. Collecting will be easy should you run behind on your payments."

I swallowed. "I'd prefer to pay on time."

Her eyes narrowed, and her mouth tightened into an evil grin. "Then your first payment is due right now."

We went upstairs, and I paid up.

57

After the ravishing, I managed to get my Jell-O-like body out of the bed, into the shower, and into the car. My mind was clear, but it felt like I'd run two marathons back-to-back.

Making babies was hard work.

I'd called Belinda and asked her to meet me at the soccer offices. She'd sounded despondent on the phone, and I thought she assumed I was just coming by to tell her that I didn't have good news and that we should go ahead and cancel the games.

When I handed her the check, she didn't say anything for five minutes. She just stared at it, her brow furrowed, like it was written in a foreign language.

"This is from some Greek place," she finally said. "I don't understand."

"You don't need to understand," I said. "But trust me when I tell you that is your money. Every penny. It went on a ride, but that is the money that belongs to Rose Petal soccer."

She stared at it some more. "Do I even wanna know?"

"No. Probably not. And it doesn't matter. The money is back, so the season is on. And I'm pretty sure the trophies are back in place now, too."

She looked at me like I was nuts. "I was over there yesterday morning. It was still empty."

"Check again today," I said. "Pretty sure they'll be there."

Moises had assured me that he and Elliott were taking them straight to the storage space at the fields. They were going to unload them, return the U-Haul, and head to Elliott's place. And probably try to figure out what to do next. I'd told them to hold tight until they heard from me. If my plan worked the way I wanted it to, they'd have to wait only a couple of days.

"Wow," Belinda said, pushing the stringy hair away from her face. "I . . . don't know what to say."

"Say the games are on."

She smiled. "The games are on."

I smiled back. "Good. Carly will be thrilled, and so will about a thousand other kids."

"What about Moises?" she asked, the smile dimming.

"He's okay."

"Oh, I don't care if he's okay. If he's got a rattlesnake in his pants and his hands are tied behind his back, I'm okay with that."

"He does not have a rattlesnake in his pants."

"Was he the one that stole the money?"

I hesitated. "Yes."

"And the trophies?"

"Yes."

She shook her head. "Incredible."

"Can I make a suggestion?"

"You found my money. You can do whatever you'd like, Deuce."

I nodded. "I don't think you should press charges."

"He stole, Deuce," she said. "Money. And trophies. All told, it was like a hundred grand in cash and prizes."

"I know. But you have it all back now."

"So that makes it all right?" She shook her head. "No way. That weasel nearly gave me a heart attack."

"But you have it all back, and you didn't have a heart attack," I said, trying to get her to come around. "Everything is okay. I'm not sure what good comes from punishing him."

"How about the fact that he might not be able to steal again?" she said.

"I don't think he will."

"If he's in jail, you won't have to think. You'll know."

I sighed. "Belinda. Come on."

"I'm not following you, Deuce. At all. I know you're one heckuva nice guy, but I'm not understanding why you would let this turkey walk."

"You're pissed at him," I said. "And justifiably so. But he's genuinely sorry. Really. And we got everything back." I paused. "I don't wanna go into the details, but the guy's had a rough go of it. Most of it his fault, but not all of it. I don't excuse what he did. But I guess I'm asking you not to make it worse for him."

She flipped the check over in her hands a couple of times, frowning at me. I understood her conflict.

If I was in her shoes, I'd probably have felt the same way. I was not sure why I was so sympathetic to Moe, but I thought it went back to feeling like the guy got bullied and no one wanted to help him. Or maybe didn't know how to help him. I just didn't see what good would come from locking him up. He wasn't so much a criminal as a guy who'd made some really horrific decisions because he was afraid. More than anything, I thought he needed some friends and some support.

"He can't be on the board anymore," Belinda said, setting the check down on the desk.

"Of course. I know that, and so does he."

"He know you're here?"

"No. I'm doing this on my own."

She nodded slowly. "Okay. He literally can't be involved with the programs at all. Ever again. I won't bend on that."

"That's fair."

"And I want an apology from him," she said. "To my face."

"I can arrange that."

She let out a sigh, still clearly torn. It was like she wanted to come up with something that I'd disagree with so she could go after him. Again, I didn't begrudge her those feelings. They were fair and understandable.

"Fine," she said. "If the trophies are back, I won't press charges."

"Thank you."

"And I'll figure out how to get you and your partner paid this next week."

"Don't worry about it," I said. "You're not pressing

charges. I know that's not an easy thing. Consider us square."

"I don't wanna do that, Deuce," she said. "You seriously saved the season. We owe you."

"We're good," I told her. "Really. I appreciate you letting this go. That's enough."

She frowned at me.

"I'm not gonna take your money," I said. "So don't try."

"What about your partner?"

I pictured an "already irritated with me" Victor when I told him we'd just done this whole thing for free.

"He'll be fine," I lied.

58

I spent the next two days putting the last pieces of my plan together. A couple of calls to Victor, a call to Myrtle Callaghan to let her know we were on track, a call to Moises and Elliott to assure them I hadn't forgotten them, and clearing my Sunday morning.

"Do I need to set aside bail money for you?" Julianne asked once or twice.

"Nothing illegal and nothing that illicit," I said. "I promise."

"I don't want Daddy to go to jail!" Carly yelled. "Who would make me breakfast?"

The love of a child.

The games went on as planned on Saturday. The Mighty, Fightin', Tiny Mermaids came together and laid a 6–2 whupping on the Purple Ladybugs. Belinda waved at me during the game and seemed happy to be patrolling the fields once again.

On Sunday morning I got up early, showered, put on some dress slacks and a button-down shirt, kissed Julianne good-bye, and told her I'd be back in time for a late breakfast. She murmured something, rolled over, and fell back to sleep.

I guess I'd convinced her I wouldn't be arrested anytime soon.

The traffic around New Spirit Fellowship Church was akin to a sporting event or a rock concert. Police officers directed traffic in the clogged streets leading to the massive parking lot, guiding us in and waving, happy to see us. Volunteers wearing bright orange vests smiled as they directed us into parking spots and welcomed us with loud shouts of "Good morning!"

I walked with the throngs toward the church. It was a balanced mix of families, seniors, and single people. The doors were held by more volunteers, all wearing shiny name tags, greeting us as we stepped through the doors.

I hadn't stepped foot inside the church when I'd brought Carly to camp, so I had to stop for a second and take it all in when I walked inside.

It was the size of an arena. A massive stage at the front, two huge screens hanging above it, balcony seating overhead. I quickly estimated that it held close to six thousand people, and the seats were filling fast. It had all the intimacy of a college football game.

Haygood knew how to put on a show.

I settled into a seat on the lower level and waited for the show to start.

The floodlights above the stage flickered, and a ripple of excitement worked its way through the crowd. There was movement in the shadows of the stage, and then the floodlights above the stage flashed on and the band illuminated in the lights roared into a loud, raucous . . . hymn.

The congregation rose to their feet, clapping and

raising their hands, rocking and swaying to the music. The band was young, hip, dressed in ripped-up jeans and T-shirts, hair spiked up, their arms covered in bracelets. They were indistinguishable from any young band you might see on YouTube.

The lyrics were tough to distinguish, but I had to admit, the band was good.

The song ended, and the congregation applauded and then went into a frenzy when Charles Haygood strode out onto the stage, waving like a newly elected president. He wore expensive-looking blue jeans and a long-sleeve button-down and a wireless mic that wrapped around his cheek.

He motioned for the crowd to settle down, and he opened with a blessing, invoking Jesus, God, and several other things that I missed because I was just confused that anyone would consider this a church service. It had been years since I'd been in a Sunday service, but this was a far cry from what I remembered.

The hour-long service moved quickly. Lots of songs and lots of Haygood telling us about honesty and how honesty wasn't always easy, but it was the way to becoming closer to God.

Ironic.

There was also a fifteen-minute period where baskets were passed, and lots and lots and lots of money went from people's pockets into the baskets.

I declined.

The service ended with another rip-roaring number from the band, and the excited congregation filed out, happy and smiling and ready to go be honest.

Haygood was already in the middle of the vestibule

as people streamed out, receiving members of his congregation as they exited and kissed up to him. I let the line thin out before I walked toward him.

His radiant smile remained as he stuck his hand out in my direction. "Mr. Winters. So nice to see you on a Sunday morning. I guess your daughter convinced you this might be a fun place?"

"Not exactly," I said, shaking his hand. "I was hoping I might be able to have a few minutes of your time."

"As you can see, Sundays are pretty busy for me," he said, chuckling.

"Yeah. Clearly. But it's about what we spoke about before. The money?"

He raised his eyebrows. "Do you have news?"

"I do."

"Give me a few minutes, and we'll head up to my office."

I stood to the side as he continued to schmooze his followers. Twenty minutes later, he motioned to me and we headed up to his massive office.

"I take it you found Mr. Huber?" he said, sliding into same chair he'd sat in before and offering the other one to me.

"I did."

"And where was he?"

"In a bit of trouble," I said, not interested in sharing details with him. "But he's okay now."

"Do the authorities have him in custody?"

"No."

"Ah. I probably need to file a complaint for that to happen," he said, nodding. "I will do that today."

"I don't think that would be a great idea."

He looked at me, surprised. "No?"

"No."

"Well, then, I guess I'm confused."

"I was, too," I said. "Until I talked with Moises."

"Did he tell you more lies?" He chuckled, shaking his head.

"No. I don't think he did."

The room got quiet. He waited for me to say something else, but I was happy to wait him out.

"I'm not quite sure why you're here, then," he said. "Have you recovered the money that belonged to me?"

"I actually recovered something better," I said. I reached into my back pocket and pulled out a small folded envelope. I held it out to him.

He took it. "Is this a check?"

"Hardly."

He hesitated, then opened the envelope. He pulled out the pictures, and his face went pale.

I smiled.

"What is this?" he said.

"You want me to explain it to you?"

He didn't say anything.

"Okay, I will," I said, shrugging. "That is a giant estate out near the lake."

I'd purposely given him only a picture of the house, not any of the woman. I didn't think the infidelity was any of my business. That was his problem. And I didn't think I needed to mention her to get what I wanted from him.

His face reddened, and a snarl started to form on his mouth.

"He didn't take the money," I said. "You did. And you tried to blame him."

"You don't know that."

"Pretty sure I do. So, no. I don't have your money. You still have it. But you're going to give it to me."

His face went purple. "Excuse me?"

"Actually, you're right. It's not your money. It's the church's money. And I don't think the people in your flock would appreciate learning that their contributions went toward building your second home."

Every inch of skin tightened on his face.

"So here's what I'm going to suggest," I said. "First, I need sixty thousand dollars in cash. Not for me, but to pay back some people. Think of it as a donation."

I almost sensed relief in his face, and I knew that was because I wasn't asking for the half million he'd told me had been stolen. He walked over to a cabinet, opened it, and popped open the door on a small safe inside. He reached in, did some counting, and then closed the safe and the cabinet.

He set a fat yellow envelope on the table. "There you go."

"Great. Now let's talk about doing some work for the community."

He raised an eyebrow.

"I want you to make a donation. Specifically, to something like, say, youth soccer. I'd suggest the Rose Petal Youth Soccer Association," I said. "Do it publicly and take the credit. I really don't care. And let me suggest an amount. Maybe half a million dollars? How does that sound?"

His face reddened. "Like hell I will."

"We can say 'hell' in a church?"

"I'm not giving you anything."

"Well, that's certainly your choice," I said. "Absolutely your choice. But I'm pretty sure your congregation would be frustrated to learn their money had gone anywhere other than the church."

He looked away.

"Message boards can be brutal," I said. "Who knows what people might start putting out there about you and your church? Because they'll find out. People always do."

He stared at his feet, quiet. I wasn't sure what he was thinking about, but I didn't want to interrupt his reverie or prayer or whatever it was.

"I'll get the check to the soccer association by Friday," he said.

"Excellent!"

"I want all the photos."

I pulled out the flash drive Victor had given me. He had sat outside the farm for an hour two nights earlier and had got the photos we needed. Haygood was very predictable.

I tossed him the drive, and he caught it, clutching it to his chest.

"Don't ever set foot in my church again," he growled.

I stood. "That won't be a problem."

"And one day I'll be coming for you," he said, pointing a finger at me. "You will pay for this."

I smiled at him as I walked to the door. I opened it and turned to him.

"I thought you'd feel better about this," I said.

He looked perplexed. "What?"

"All this honesty," I said. "I thought it would make you feel better."

59

I walked outside, and Myrtle Callaghan was standing next to my car.

I handed her the envelope.

"That was easy," she said.

"If you say so."

"Hey, if you ever are looking for another job, I'm always looking for good investigators who can—"

"Not ever," I said. "Not ever."

60

I drove home, relieved. It was over.

I needed to make a few calls to let Victor know it was really done and to figure out what I was gonna have to do to make everything up to him. I needed to call Moises and Elliott to let them know they were in the clear so they could figure out how to start their lives again.

And I just needed some time at home with my girls.

I parked the van in the driveway and bounded into the house, ready for a Sunday with nothing but family.

"Anyone home?" I called to the empty living room.

"In here, Daddy!" Carly yelled.

She was parked on the sofa, eyes glued to an over-size picture book.

"Where's Mom?"

"Upstairs. She was taking a shower."

I gave her a quick kiss on the cheek before bounding up the stairs.

I found Julianne in our bedroom, sitting on our bed, legs crossed Indian style.

"Are we having a powwow?" I asked, smiling.

Julianne smiled. "Not quite."

"Are you sick?" Julianne never sat still. Ever.

She shook her head. There were tears in the corners of her eyes, but she was smiling. "No."

I was confused. "What? What is it?"

She held up her hand.

She was holding up what looked like a small Popsicle stick.

And there was a bright pink plus sign on it.

Keep reading for a special sneak peek at
Father Knows Death,
the next Stay at Home Dad Mystery
featuring Deuce Winters. . . .

1

George Spellman's lifeless face gazed at me amid the packages of frozen bratwursts.

I stared at him for a moment and then closed the freezer door. Not because I was shocked or horrified at finding a dead body. I closed it because I realized I wasn't fazed by finding a dead man stuffed inside a freezer. I wondered if I should just stop opening things.

It was late April, and I was working the grill at the Carriveau County Fair. Carly had joined our local 4-H chapter last year, and one of their big fund-raisers was working the food stand during the fair. Nothing quite like working an outdoor grill in a hundred-and-five-degree heat.

"I think we're gonna need some more, Deuce," Harlan Boodle said, wiping his brow with a red bandanna. "Lunch rush is gonna be any minute."

The large grill was littered with thin hamburger patties, hot dogs, and a few bratwursts. They were probably seasoned with a bit of Harlan's sweat.

"There's a big freezer in the back," he said, pointing

toward the kitchen. "We use it for extra storage. Should be a bunch in there."

"How many should I grab?" I asked.

"As many as you can carry," he said, chuckling. "It's gonna be a madhouse in about five minutes."

We'd been working nonstop since our four-hour shift began, and I found it hard to believe it could get any busier. I could think of about fifty other things I would've rather been doing on a Saturday afternoon than basting myself over a dirty grill at our county fair. One thing you learn as a parent is that when your kid signs up for something, you're signing up for something, too.

"All right," I told Harlan. "Be back in a minute."

"Grab us some drinks, too." He flipped the already overdone patties again. "So we don't die out here."

I waved at him and stepped into the food stand kitchen, which was nothing more than a sauna-like shack that disguised itself as a fast-food restaurant for one week a year. There was a covered eating area for about a hundred people, front and back counters, a giant indoor grill, some sinks, and a bunch of refrigerators.

Oh, and about fifty people squeezed into the kitchen, trying to serve the fairgoers.

Voices screamed and yelled about cheese and drinks and burgers and buns as people who had no business serving and preparing food attempted to do just that.

A pink-faced Carly squeezed by me, carrying two bottles of water. "Hey, Daddy."

"What's up, kid?"

"I'm getting water," she shouted. "For some people!"

Her oversize green shirt hung nearly to her knees,

and her hair was hidden beneath a bright yellow bandanna.

"Good for you, kiddo."

She scurried past me and snaked her way through the group of workers out to the front counter to deliver her water.

Julianne was perched on a tall stool, her hands submerged in a deep sink, washing trays.

I walked over and kissed her sweaty cheek. "You should probably be at home."

She spun on the stool to look at me. Her green T-shirt was riding up over her enormous stomach.

"Why?" she asked, setting down a tray. "Because it's seven hundred degrees in here and I'm, like, fourteen months pregnant?"

"Yes. Exactly."

"I'm tough."

I touched her very round belly. "I know that. I'm just hoping the new kid likes the heat."

"They won't have a choice. We live in Texas, Deuce."

"Doesn't mean you need to boil them in your stomach."

"I'm hoping it will encourage it to get the hell out of my body," she said.

She was a week past her due date and looked ready to pop. Because I enjoyed my health, I didn't say that out loud. But she'd been carrying around a baby for ten months now, and she was ready to bond with it in person. We all were.

"I'm going to get sausages," I said.

"Oh, great. I'll just stay here and wash trays and be enormous."

"And beautiful."

"Ha. Good one, sausage boy."

I kissed her again. "I love you."

"And I want this kid out of me, and I swear to God, I'll have it right in this disgusting kitchen if I need to," she said, spinning back on the stool. "Oh, and I love you, too."

Pregnant women are funny.

I wound my way through the back of the kitchen, my thoughts focused on babies instead of sausages. I was excited that the baby was going to be there any day. Carly was, too. We were all ready to meet the newest member of the Winters family. We had no idea whether it was a boy or a girl. Julianne had insisted on not knowing. I had protested greatly. And it didn't matter even a little.

"Babies should be a surprise," she said. "Like presents on Christmas. Plus, it's in my stomach, so I get to decide."

Which was a hard point to argue with.

I liked seeing her pregnant. Not miserable, though, and with the summer heat, I knew she was pretty uncomfortable. But I did have this fear that her water was going to break right in the middle of the dinner rush, and that would be some sort of health code violation.

And so I was thinking about babies and rushing to the hospital when I opened the freezer and saw George Spellman's dead face among the bratwursts.

And after thinking that I needed to stop opening things, my next thought was that a dead body in the freezer was probably a far worse health code violation than having a baby in the kitchen.

2

"Well, this isn't good," Matilda Biggs said, shaking her head.

The technicians were loading the body into the back of the ambulance, and the police had formed a barricade around the back of the food stand. Matilda, a member of the fair board, was concerned.

"This is really going to reflect poorly on the fair," she said. "Could drive down revenue."

"Uh, yeah," I said, less concerned about revenue than I was for George's family.

"I mean, Iron Horse plays tomorrow night," she said, staring at me. "We're expecting a big crowd. Huge. It wouldn't be good if we had to cancel that."

I didn't know Matilda well, but I knew of her. She was hard not to know of because she was hard to miss.

She was nearly four hundred pounds.

And that wasn't one of those exaggerated statements about someone carrying a few extra pounds. She was one of the biggest women I'd ever seen. She was just short of six feet and seemingly almost as wide, with rolls of fat billowing from every part of her body. I'd only ever seen her wearing black sweats and some sort of stretched-out T-shirt, as I assumed she wasn't able to find anything else to fit her enormous body. Her stringy black hair was thinning on top and stuck to the sides of her head with sweat. She was never more than a few feet away from her golf cart, as that was the only way she was able to make it around the fairgrounds.

She pulled a walkie-talkie from her hip and punched a button. "Mama, this is Matilda. You copy? Over."

Five seconds later, the walkie-talkie crackled.

"This is Mama. Roger that, I copy. Over."

Mama was not code for some motherly figure in Matilda's life. Mama was Mama. Her mother. Who worked right alongside her on the fair board. I didn't know the specifics, but I was pretty sure everyone on the entire fair board was somehow related to one another.

"We're gonna need a new freezer," Matilda said. "The police are telling me we can't use this one, on account of Deuce Winters finding George Spellman in it. Over."

The Rose Petal Police had, in fact, cordoned off the large freezer with yellow crime-scene tape.

"Roger. I'm already on it," Mama said through the walkie-talkie. "I've got another one on the way. Should be there in about fifteen minutes. Over."

Matilda nodded. "Ten-four." She stuck the walkie-talkie back on her hip. "I gotta make some calls. Make sure we got more sausages coming."

She waddled over to the golf cart, dropped in behind the steering wheel, and took off, spraying dirt and weeds behind her.

Carly and Julianne made their way around the food stand building to me. Carly surveyed the scene, trying to take everything in. I resisted the urge to pull the bandanna from her hair to her eyes.

Julianne just raised her eyebrows. "Well, this is interesting. You already talk to the police?"

"Yeah. Took all of five minutes. I didn't do anything other than open the freezer door."

"Maybe this time you won't be a suspect."

I narrowed my eyes. "Very funny."

She shrugged. "You sort of have a way of falling into these things."

It was hard to deny that, as much as I might've liked to. My part-time private-investigating gig existed only because I kept finding myself embroiled in the criminal activity in Rose Petal. Julianne had made several subtle suggestions that, with a new baby on the way, maybe I might want to curtail my activity in that arena. I didn't disagree.

But it seemed that trouble was still finding me, no matter how much I tried to avoid it.

As I contemplated that, Susan Blamunski hustled our way.

"Oh, good Lord," Julianne whispered. "Red alert. Crazy woman dead ahead."

Susan's face was a mask of concern.

And heavy eye make-up.

"Deuce," she said, grabbing me by the elbow. "What is going *on*?"

I tried to casually shake free from the grasp of our local 4-H leader but failed. "I'm not completely sure."

"I heard they found a dead body," she said. She glanced at Julianne and, for the first time, seemed to notice she was there. "Oh, hello, Julianne. So nice to see you. We rarely get the opportunity to see you at four-H events."

The corners of Julianne's mouth twitched. "Hello, Susan."

"So nice that your entire family could work the fair," she said to me. "Finally."

"We worked it last year," Julianne said through gritted teeth.

"Did you?" Susan asked, pursing her lips. "I don't recall. Seems like we see you so . . . infrequently."

If Julianne had access to a hammer, I was pretty sure she would've used it on Susan's skull at that moment. The fact that Julianne was in the process of establishing her own law practice after leaving her firm earlier in the year meant she was having to put in some serious hours before the baby was born.

But Susan's digs about our family were nothing we hadn't heard before. Our nontraditional family was still a novelty in Rose Petal. People couldn't seem to get used to the role reversal we'd chosen in our home. It worked just fine for us, but there was no doubt that we were the topic of much conversation throughout town.

Julianne took Carly's hand. "Come on, baby. Let's go check out the bunnies. Before they have another dead body to deal with."

If Susan picked up on the fact that she was the potential other body, she didn't show it.

"When is she due?" she asked.

"Supposed to be a week ago," I said. "Any day now."

"That explains her size," she murmured. She tugged on her own green shirt, smoothing it over her modest stomach.

She refocused on the activity around us. "So, I heard they found some man in the freezer?"

"Yeah, George Spellman."

"And you found him?"

"Yeah."

She squeezed my elbow. "How terrible! Why was he in there?"

"Uh, I don't know. I just found him."

Her concern now outweighed her make-up. "This isn't going to be good. Did they say anything about the food stand?"

"Not yet."

"We get nearly all of our funding from this week," she said. "Without it, we won't have any money for activities. For anything."

That was the truth. The food stand was the major fund-raiser each year for our local 4-H. Nothing else brought in money even comparable.

"I'm sure the police will be done soon." I wasn't sure at all, but it seemed like a good way to placate her.

Susan looked around the area. "And didn't I see Matilda over here earlier?"

"Yeah, she was here," I said. "But I think she went to go find out about the new freezer or something."

Susan's lips tied together. "Well, that's interesting."

"What? That she went to find a new freezer?"

"No, no," Susan said, lowering her voice. She looked up at me like she was about to share the most earth-shattering secret in the world with me. "I heard something . . . interesting."

"You keep using that word."

She glanced around me before settling her eyes on mine. "I heard that she was having an affair with the dead man."

3

I wasn't sure I'd heard correctly.

"Matilda??"

Susan nodded her head, her hairspray-drenched curls bobbing obediently. "Yes. She and George. Everyone is talking about it."

I was pretty sure the only person talking about it was Susan. And if other people were talking about it, it was because of her.

"Hmm. That is . . . interesting."

She waited for me to ask questions. I didn't.

"Don't you want to know?" she asked. "I thought you were an 'investigator.'"

"I am. But I'm not working this case." Or any case at the moment. Which was pretty much fine with me.

"You might want to after you hear about Matilda."

She wasn't gonna stop. "Fine. What makes you think they were having an affair?"

Susan pulled me away from the food stand, toward the arts and crafts building. I wasn't sure why. It wasn't as if people were crowding around, gawking at the crime scene. George's body had been removed, and the police cars were gone. One car was still parked next to the building, a dark blue, unmarked sedan. The detective working the case.

She stopped just short of the entrance to the arts and crafts building and pulled me next to the wall.

"I saw them," she whispered. "Together."

I flinched. I wasn't so sure I wanted more details about four-hundred-pound Matilda and her supposed lover.

"At Texas Roadhouse," she continued, and I breathed a sigh of relief.

"You saw them at dinner?" I said. "I'm sure they were friends, Susan. George was the groundskeeper here."

George Spellman operated a small lawn service business in Rose Petal. He also moonlighted as the groundskeeper at the Carriveau County fairgrounds during the summer.

Susan shook her head. "No. This was not a business dinner."

I'll admit, I was curious. "How do you know?"

Her fingernails dug into my forearm. "There were tears. She was clutching his arm. I think . . . I think he might have been leaving her. Ending the relationship."

This was a woman who watched far too many soap operas.

"You know, people might say the same thing about me and you," I said.

Her lipstick-reddened mouth formed a perfect O. "Oh?"

I glanced at my arm. "You just pulled me away from a crowd. You're whispering into my ear. Clutching my arm . . ."

She dropped my arm like it was a stick crawling with fire ants.

"Deuce Winters! I am insulted!" She stepped away, the picture of indignation.

"Just sayin'." I tried not to laugh. "Look, I gotta go find my wife. Make sure she doesn't hear any rumors about me and you."

Susan glared after me as I walked away.

Julianne and Carly were in the animal barn, along with a sea of other fairgoers. It wasn't air-conditioned, but there were fans circulating hot air, at least giving the impression that people were being cooled off.

"Is the viper gone?" Julianne sat perched on a tiny chair, her stomach ballooning in front of her. I wasn't sure if she'd be able to get up.

"Yeah, she's gone."

"Daddy, look at this bunny!" Carly sat across from Julianne, the biggest rabbit I'd ever seen huddled in her lap.

"Are you sure that isn't a bear?" I asked. I stroked the rabbit's silky ears.

"I want him," she told me. "He's for sale. The sign on the cage says so. He's only ten dollars!"

"And he probably eats ten dollars worth of food a day," I said.

"Daddy," Carly said, scolding me. "He's not *that* big." She stood to return him to his cage.

"What else did Susan have to say?" Julianne asked.

I stood behind her and rubbed her shoulders. "The usual. Just some rumors about the dead guy."

"What kind of rumors?"

"That he and Matilda were having an affair."

Julianne whipped her head around to look at me. "Are you serious?"

"Serious that she said that? Yes. Serious that he was? Good God, I hope not."

"Deuce." Her voice was filled with warning.

"What?"

"Do not get involved."

"I don't intend to."

"That's not good enough."

She pushed on the seat of the chair, trying to heave herself to a standing position. I grabbed her under the shoulders and helped.

"I mean it," she said, her eyes narrowed. "I am a hundred weeks pregnant. I am about to have a baby. I have a practice that needs all of my time and then some. *Do not get involved.*"

I held her to me. "Okay, okay." I kissed the top of her head.

"Promise me."

"I promise."